# CHASING

KYLIE GILMORE

Chasing: © 2021 by Kylie Gilmore

Cover design by: Michele Catalano Creative

Published by: Extra Fancy Books

ISBN-13: 978-1-64658-031-6

*It's all about the chase.*

# 1

*Paige*

Day three of the never-ending holiday weekend from hell will not break me. I'm tough. I'm strong.

I'm losing it.

The inn I co-own with my sister Brooke is fully booked, and I'm on my own for the first time for the long Fourth of July weekend. I'm on the deck, keeping an eye on a rowdy kid who seems determined to get food all over the inn's brand-new furniture. Don't get me wrong, I love kids. Just not the messy kind.

Normally I wouldn't be so frazzled, but I've barely slept the past two nights. Why? Oh, no biggie. Just a wedding invitation from my ex-fiancé. And it arrived on my thirtieth birthday! The big 3-0. My eggs are shriveling by the minute, along with my youth. I reach for my fourth chocolate chip cookie and take a ferocious bite. *Die, cheating ex!*

I'm counting the seconds until I can open that Shiraz meant for just such an occasion—when the man who bailed the week before your wedding to run off with a flight attendant is now marrying her. I haven't seen Noah in two years, but this invitation reopened the wound.

I could accept that he left me because he's a cheater incapable of commitment, yet here he is committing to someone else. I blink back tears, reaching for righteous anger instead.

Seriously, who sends a wedding invitation to their ex-fiancée? Pure arrogance. I gave him four prime years of my twenties when I could've been out there meeting other, better men. Worse, I fit myself into *his* life and looked past his womanizing reputation to believe in the fairy tale. Not that I'm bitter. Much.

And to top off the never-ending weekend from hell, I have to deal with another arrogant man, our caterer, Spencer Wolf. He's around my age, tall with close-cropped light brown hair, blue eyes with thick lashes I would kill for, and a scruffy square jaw. Besides the fact that he flirts shamelessly with any woman with a pulse, including both me and my sister *at the same time*, the biggest problem with Spencer is that he thinks he's the boss when *I'm* the boss. *Grr…*

I glance toward the kitchen window, considering checking on him. I have to keep on top of him, or he goes a different way than we agreed to, coming up with menu items we never discussed and dropping others completely. Honestly, I don't know why I put up with him.

I catch his eye accidentally, and he salutes me. *Cocky jerk.* I turn away.

Ten-year-old Joey runs by with his melting chocolate ice-cream cone, heading toward the back door of the inn. I rush after him. The last thing I need is chocolate stains all over the beige living room furniture. "Joey, wait! Ice cream is outside food." His parents bought ice cream in town at Summerdale Sweets before coming back to the inn for a barbecue. Why didn't they make their kids finish their cones at the shop?

"He has to use the bathroom," his mom calls from the lower patio.

I catch up to him and block the back door with my body. "I'll hold your ice cream for you." *Why doesn't his mom step in here?* I look over at her, but she's smiling at something her husband is saying, looking all lovey-dovey, and I don't want to spoil the moment for them. Word of mouth is crucial for the inn.

Joey scowls. "Carla took her ice cream with her."

I wince. "Is she inside?"

"Yup. She had to get her stupid mermaid from her suitcase."

*Why???* I should've wrapped all the furniture in plastic.

"I'll hold yours," I say in a firm tone. "It's not sanitary to take food into the bathroom." *Which your parents should care about!*

"No way, lady. You'll lick it."

A large male hand appears from just over my shoulder. I didn't even hear the back door open. "Hand it over, little man. You can make your own sundae after dinner. Much better than a soggy cone." It's Spencer. I step to the side to let him do his man-to-little-man thing. Spencer's tone is coaxing, but the rest of his broad-shouldered authoritative self indicates there will be no argument.

"With chocolate syrup?" Joey asks him.

Spencer ruffles his hair, and my ovaries do a happy dance. *Dad material.*

Also, my ovaries are traitors. *We don't like Spencer, girls!*

"That's right," Spencer says. "Homemade. I'll even let you lick the chocolate syrup spoon after I'm done."

"Swear?" Joey asks.

Spencer crosses his heart solemnly. My own heart squeezes.

"Deal!" Joey hands him the cone and dashes inside.

Spencer steps outside with the cone, his blue eyes sparkling as they meet mine. I fight the urge to hug him. A rare blush heats my cheeks at the thought, and my pulse quickens. *Whoa. What is happening right now?* He's luring me in with his dad potential and sparkling eyes.

Okay, just because Spencer was unexpectedly good with one kid doesn't make him special or extra hot. At least not any hotter than usual. I mean, yes, objectively speaking, he's good looking. Doesn't mean I'm attracted to him. It's what's on the inside that counts.

"Sucker," Spencer says in a conspiratorial tone. "I'm

totally going to lick his ice cream." He pretends to chomp down on the cone and tosses it into the nearby garbage.

"Thanks, you were great with him." My voice sounds breathy. *Chill.*

His brows lift at the compliment. "I confiscated Carla's cone when she ran inside for her mermaid doll. You really should keep a better eye on your pint-sized guests."

If I weren't so sleep deprived, I'd have a wicked comeback. This is what we do—give each other a hard time. Instead I just stare at him, mutely grateful and a little mushy over his way with kids.

Then he ruins it. "By the way, I wasn't happy with the sweet corn, so I switched over to vegetable skewers. The guests will love it."

He swaggers back inside to the kitchen to prepare food I didn't authorize. Again.

Hold on now, I paid for sweet corn; the guests expect sweet corn. I follow him inside, where he's making quick work of chopping peppers.

"Where's the sweet corn?" I ask.

"In the compost pile."

*Wasting food and money.* My sister and I only opened the inn a month ago. It's my only source of income, and we both poured our life savings into it. I can't afford regular losses, especially when we're not fully booked for the summer, which is supposed to be our high season.

I plant my hands on my hips. "We've covered this before. We work out a menu and that's that. I printed it out and put it in every guest's room. It's on our website and all our holiday advertising. Half the reason they wanted to be here for the Fourth of July was that menu."

"They're here for my cooking, and that's what they'll get." He grabs a large onion and makes short work of chopping that up for the skewers. He's a pro. He doesn't even cry from the fumes.

I admit he's a great chef, which is the only reason we hired him. Brooke twisted my arm on that one. There really wasn't anyone close to his level of skill in the area, and he was willing to work on the occasional basis we need him. Mostly for wedding receptions and holidays. Normally, he's the chef at The Horseman Inn in town.

Still, I can't let him walk all over me. Why have a menu if he's going to go rogue every time? The Inn on Lovers' Lane has two things that make it stand out from all the other B&Bs in the area—great food and elopement wedding packages. We went the romantic route to attract couples since we already had the romantic name from our location on Lovers' Lane. It was mostly my younger sister Kayla's idea, who loves planning weddings and all things romance. Men don't romance me. They probably don't see me as the type who'd fall all over them in appreciation. Just saying, it would be nice.

I give Spencer my best *I'm in charge here* look. "You can't just throw out food. I paid for that fresh from the farmers' market yesterday. It couldn't have been that bad."

He doesn't even glance up from his work. "Executive decision. Next time let me pick up the ingredients. You don't know what to look for."

"It looked good! I even peeked under the husks. Every single one."

"Meh."

I bristle. "I'm in charge here. *I* make the executive decisions."

"Do you, though?" He doesn't wait for my reply, merely shifts to retrieve a large colander of washed mushrooms.

"I sign your paycheck," I remind him.

He chops the mushrooms neatly in halves. "Because you need the best chef in town. Why do you think every review about the inn mentions the food?"

"I'm the one who makes the breakfast guests rave about."

"Which is my menu that I taught you and Brooke to make." He points his knife at me. "Face it, Paige, you'd be lost without me, so instead of arguing over menu items, why don't you mosey along, put a big smile on that crabby face, and make sure your guests are happy. Isn't that *your* job?"

I sputter. "I know my job!"

"Then why aren't you doing it?"

I toss my hands in the air. "Ergh!"

He barks out a laugh. "Right back at ya."

"This is the last time I hire you for a gig," I mutter on my way out.

"Keep telling yourself that. We both know you can't resist me."

I push open the back door and give him one last glare over my shoulder.

He flashes a wolfish grin that sends an unexpected shiver of excitement down my spine. I turn abruptly and walk outside. Nothing exciting about a wolf. Spencer Wolf. It suits him.

I put a hand to the side of my neck where my pulse beats wildly. Danger is not the same thing as excitement. Not at all.

~

*Spencer*

I'm not sure why I keep taking these side gigs for the witchiest woman I've ever met. Sure, Paige is beautiful with her tousled wavy brown hair, cute upturned nose, and pouty lips, but I've always preferred sweet *agreeable* women. They let me have my way. Paige fights me at every turn. It's like she doesn't get that I'm my own boss. No one, not even a client, ever bosses me.

Okay, I know why I put up with her. Money. My goal is to one day own my own restaurant. Right now I'm a chef with catering gigs on the side.

Time for my paycheck. I scan the people gathered on the inn's patio and deck. I don't see Paige with the guests like she usually is, so I leave my two assistants to finish the cleanup outside for the grill and tables and slip inside the inn. The woman keeps a close eye on everything I do. You'd think after this, my third gig for the inn, one of which was for her younger sister Brooke's wedding reception, she'd chill about my work. I'm a master in the kitchen, using the freshest ingredients farm to table. Sometimes that means altering a menu if I'm not satisfied with the quality of an ingredient but hey.

Don't hear any of the guests complaining when they chow down. Only Paige is upset when I deviate from the expected menu. Bow to the master or do it yourself, I like to say. That goes over well with the witchy one.

I glance around the kitchen with its top-of-the-line appliances. I appreciate that Paige and Brooke went modern in the kitchen when they renovated this old Dutch farmhouse into an inn. She's not here. I continue on to the living room with its wide plank hardwood floors and overstuffed beige couches and armchairs. Empty. She's probably up in her second-floor apartment in the addition. Hopefully, she's writing out my check right now.

I hear a door open behind me and turn back to the kitchen.

Paige steps out of the walk-in pantry and startles when she sees me, her hand over her heart. Her hair is mussed, but her white floral blouse and pink skirt look pristine. Doesn't look like a guy was hiding in there with her. "You surprised me."

I'm about to razz her about hiding in the pantry when I realize she's been crying. Her face is splotchy, and her nose is red. "You okay?"

She shakes her head and strides past me, helping herself to a glass of water at the sink. "I'm fine," she says over the rush of water.

*Right.*

She takes a drink, keeping her back to me.

It's not my place to pry. Still, I'm curious. I never imagined Paige *could* cry. She wears her pride like a coat of armor. "What happened?"

She turns to face me, her chin jutting out. "Nothing. Everything go okay in here?"

"Yup. I just came in to collect my check."

"Mmm-hmm."

She makes no move to get it; instead she slumps back against the counter, the glass gripped tightly in her hand as she stares blankly at the floor.

I close the distance and take the glass from her hand, my

fingers brushing hers, an unexpected jolt going through me on contact. I've never gotten close enough to touch her before. Her pretty whiskey eyes are wide. I set the glass on the counter, valiantly trying to ignore that jolt. "I know you barely tolerate me, but if you tell me what's wrong, I'll fix it."

Her lips part, and I find myself leaning closer. She looks softer somehow, not her usual frosty self. And she smells delicious—vanilla and something distinctly her. A stirring of desire amps every sense up a level, and my heart kicks harder.

"What're you doing?" she asks softly.

I shift back, but it doesn't quell the desire. I tell myself to focus on the fact that she needs help. "Nothing. You seemed upset. I've never seen you hiding in the pantry to cry before."

"I wasn't hiding, and who said I was crying?" She brushes past me and strides from the room.

"You'd better be getting my check!" I call after her.

Her back goes even straighter if that's possible. "Bite me."

I smile to myself. Seems she's not too upset to spar with me. She disappears around the corner, heading to her apartment, I imagine. It's her office and her apartment. I only know this because she wouldn't let me follow her for my first paycheck because it was her "private space."

I head into the den, which is next to the addition, and take a seat in my favorite leather recliner chair, leaning back in it and stretching out my legs. I've been on my feet most of the day, preparing and then cooking the food. I like being my own boss. I like being the boss period. Take after dear old Dad that way. Too bad we could never stop butting heads long enough to actually work together. Imagine what we could've accomplished as a united front. Ha. Like that would ever happen.

I let out a breath, pushing down the guilt I always feel when I think about Dad. My whole life all I've heard is how much he wants me to go into business with him selling cars. He owns a chain of car lots. Even now that I'm established in my chosen profession, he still hasn't stopped talking about me taking over for him one day. I'm no sales guy. I love food and cooking. He never accepted what I chose to do with my life. Our relationship has been strained ever since I graduated high school and started working at a premier restaurant instead of joining him on the showroom floor. I apprenticed myself to great chefs, and now I am one. No culinary school for me. I wanted to dive right in with the best.

My mind wanders to tomorrow's menu at The Horseman Inn. I'll stop by the farmers' market in the morning. There should be an abundance of fresh tomatoes this time of year. I'll make caprese salad, for sure, some tomatoes set aside for sauces. Cherries should be coming in soon. I'll stop by the fish market too. I've got a small herb garden going at the back of the restaurant I can draw from. One day I'll have a property of my own with a huge garden, an orchard, and animals. The works. My own restaurant—Spencer's.

"All finished with cleanup," Rick says, appearing in the den with Sara. My assistants are a young married couple in their twenties. They're both elementary school teachers who take side gigs for extra cash.

How long was I sitting here daydreaming about my future restaurant? And where the hell is Paige?

"Great, thanks," I say, straightening the recliner and standing. "Appreciate your help today." I pull my wallet out and slide their checks out of the billfold, handing them each one.

"Need anything else?" Sara asks.

*My paycheck.* "That's all. You can go, thanks again."

They head out the front door. I look over toward the addition, debating going upstairs to knock on Paige's door. Did she forget I'm waiting here? Or maybe she's up there bawling her eyes out. Did something happen to Brooke? Her sister is away on her honeymoon. I can't fathom what else could possibly upset Paige other than something happening to her family. The woman is made of steel. Nothing fazes her, ever.

That's it. I'm going up there to find out what's going on and fix it.

I make my way through the hallway that leads to the addition, climb the stairs, and knock on her door. "Paige, it's Spencer."

"Go away," she says in a tired voice.

"No." I knock again, harder this time.

"I said go away!"

"I know you're in there bawling your eyes out, but some of us need to get paid." There. That should get her moving.

The door whips open a moment later, her light brown eyes flashing. "Wait here." She swivels on her heel and marches back into her apartment.

She left the door open, so I poke my head in. What a mess! Empty wine bottles and a pizza box on the coffee table. Papers scattered all over the white sofa with a yellow polka-dotted comforter thrown over one end. It's an open floor plan, so I get a peek at her desk buried under a mound of papers and the kitchen with a sink full of dirty dishes. Paige always looks so perfectly put together I never would've guessed she was a slob. I can only imagine what her bedroom looks like. Is there a bedroom? There's a closed door past the kitchen. Could be a bathroom. Maybe the sofa pulls out.

She heads toward me, and I ease back a step so it doesn't look like I was spying on her slobbiness. She hands me the check without a word.

"Do you sleep on your sofa?" I ask.

"None of your business."

That's when I notice the dark circles under her eyes. I bet she can't sleep and lies on the sofa all night, drinking wine and crying. Then she hides in the pantry to cry during the daytime. Something in the vicinity of my heart squeezes.

I soften my voice, trying for soothing. "Paige, whatever it is—"

She holds up a palm, tears springing to her eyes. "Don't!"

"Don't what?"

"Don't pity me!"

"I'm not. Obviously something's wrong. Did someone...die?"

"What? No."

"Oh, okay. That's good." I look over her shoulder at the mess and back to her weepy dark-circled eyes. "I just can't figure out what could possibly have gotten through that thick armor of yours."

"Ha! You think I have thick armor? Three days I've been crying." She jabs three fingers in the air. "And for what?"

I shrug, though I'm alarmed she's been crying for three whole days. "No idea."

"I'm thirty, did you know that?"

Before I can ask why that would make her cry for three whole days, she continues, gesturing wildly.

"Everyone I know is happily married, some of them with kids on the way. Wyatt's expecting his first child with Sydney. Brooke and Kayla will probably have kids soon, all the cousins being raised together."

Wyatt's her older brother. Brooke and Kayla are her younger sisters. I'm guessing she feels left behind?

"Hey, just because your siblings jump off a bridge—" I start.

"All of my friends in the city are married now too. I have a horrible collection of bridesmaid dresses to show for it and a few regrettable…never mind."

"Regrettable what?"

She presses her lips together.

I take a wild guess. "Hookups with groomsmen?"

Her cheeks redden, but before I can get any mileage out of that, she snaps, "You want to see the real problem?"

"Yes."

She marches back to her desk, snatches a card off it, and marches back to me, shoving it in my face. "*This!* This *stupid* invitation arrived on my thirtieth birthday."

I take it from her, unsure why she's taking such offense to it arriving on her birthday. Isn't it sort of random when things arrive in the mail? It's one of those fancy wedding invitations on thick cardstock. There's only two possible reasons she'd be upset over a wedding invitation. It's either an ex, or she's upset that she's still single at thirty. Ah, the birthday connection. And both her younger sisters got married last month. Ego crusher right there for big sis.

I rip the invitation in half.

She gasps.

I toss it in the air. "Problem solved."

"Spencer! I can't believe you did that!" She stares at the two pieces on the ground, and then the strangest thing happens—

She starts to laugh.

I grin.

She keeps laughing, tears coming out of her eyes as she clutches her stomach, overcome. "Why didn't I think of that?" she gasps out.

"You didn't get mad enough."

She wipes her eyes and picks up the two pieces from the floor, holding them up. "One little piece of paper wrecked me. This is from my ex-fiancé, who bailed a week before our wedding to run off with a flight attendant he'd literally just met. And then he invites me to their wedding? He's rubbing it in my face." She shakes the two sides of the invitation. "I should show up there and—and *spit* in his face!"

I relax now that she sounds more like her usual tough self. "And then when the minister asks if anyone objects to the marriage, you stand up and tell everyone that he's already married to you. No, even better, stick a pillow under your dress and say you're having his baby."

She smiles up at me under her lashes, and my pulse skyrockets. That sweet, sexy smile has never been aimed at me before. "You're nicer than I thought."

"Must be losing my touch," I say huskily.

"I like that objecting part. I couldn't pull off a fake pregnancy, though."

"Why not?"

"I don't think I could convincingly waddle."

I walk into her place, grab a pillow off the sofa, and stuff it under my black button-down shirt. "Observe." I do a convincing pregnant waddle around her living room.

She plants her hands on her hips. "Maybe you should say *you're* having his baby."

I chuckle and pull the pillow out, tossing it back on the sofa. "Somebody should."

She drops her hands, looking lost in thought. And then she starts muttering to herself, something about how she really needs to get out more and "passable." Is she okay now or about to fall apart? I can't walk away if she's still a sobbing mess.

"Paige?"

She walks closer and studies me intensely. A warning bell goes off in my mind. She doesn't have that soft look in her eyes anymore; now she's back to her usual take-charge demeanor. This always spells trouble between us. We can't both be the take-charge person without butting heads.

"What?" I remind myself she's going through something right now, so I should at least attempt to keep the peace.

She presses her finger to her lush lips. "I just had a crazy thought."

The hair on the back of my neck stands up. As a rule, I steer clear of other people's crazy. "Don't tell me."

"I could go to this wedding with the right date." She gives me a thorough once-over and then slowly walks around me.

I glance at her over my shoulder. "Uh, why do I suddenly feel like a piece of meat?"

She snaps her teeth at me. "Don't worry. I'm a vegetarian."

"I saw you eat a burger today."

"Just where you're concerned. You're not my type." Her expression is grimly determined, and a trickle of unease runs down my spine.

"Uh, thanks?"

"My ex sent that invitation to rub it in my face because I told him he'd never be able to commit to anyone and he'd live a long, empty life devoid of love and die alone. You know, the usual post-breakup stuff."

"As you do."

She warms to her topic, color flushing her cheeks. "He probably never expected me to attend his wedding. And I had no plans to go, but—" she holds up a finger "—now hear me out, this could actually work to my benefit. His best friend runs a media company that includes a travel magazine that likes to feature B&Bs in quaint towns. I'm sure he'll be the best man. I could go to the wedding to make that connection and really put the inn on the map. And I could network among all the influential friends Noah and I had in common and convince them to stay at the inn and spread the word. I could get a lot of business out of this wedding while also showing Noah that I'm doing awesome without him."

I see where she's going with this, and part of me wants to stick it to her ex too. Cheaters are weak with no sense of honor. And to cheat on a fiancée? Total dick move. Why bother with the commitment of marriage if you don't intend to honor it?

"So you need a date to hold your head high," I say.

Her eyes gleam. "I need better than a date. I need a husband to shove in my ex's face. Just a fake husband. That's where you come in."

I lift my brows. "Wouldn't all those friends you have in common know if you had gotten married?"

She frowns. "We haven't been in touch. Noah got all of our couple friends in the breakup. He was friends with the guys, and us girlfriends were thrown together so much we became friends too."

"They dumped you?"

Her lips form a flat line. "They didn't dump me. I graciously bowed out so as not to cause any awkwardness."

I try to picture it, but can't. "Sorry, not buying it."

Her jaw sets in that stubborn way I'm beginning to find irresistible. "You weren't there. So-o-o, will you be my fake husband at this wedding? You're the only guy I can think of who could pull it off with your, uh, supreme confidence." She gestures airily. "Honestly, I've been so busy with work I haven't met a lot of single guys lately." She stills. "You are single, aren't you? I just assumed you were because of the way you flirt with everyone."

"Not everyone. Just single women."

She shakes her head. "I'll pay you for your time. You're already on my payroll, after all. Strictly business to promote the inn." She looks at me expectantly.

"No."

Her face falls. "That's it? Just no? Hmm, what would you say to…" She trails off as I step into her personal space, sensing prime negotiating time.

The blood rushes through my veins. "I don't want your money, so I'd have to say what else could I get out of it?"

Her breath hitches, but then she must sense a negotiation too because she changes tactics. "Mmm." She examines my jaw. "I like the scruff. Keep that. Maybe grow it a little longer for a short beard. Can you do that in three weeks?"

"Easy. And again, what do I get out of it?"

Her chin lifts. "What do you want?" She holds up a finger. "Be reasonable."

My lips curve up. "Don't you know me by now, Paige? I'm not a reasonable man."

## 2

*Paige*

My heart pounds as a rush of unwanted desire floods me. Spencer's the only one I can think of who could show up my ex—arrogant player for arrogant player. And the best part is, I don't have to worry about getting tangled up with Spencer because, if the past few months of working with him have shown me anything, it's that we're completely incompatible. The plan is genius, only I didn't anticipate this desire. How can I be turned on by a bossy, arrogant man?

Spencer's blue eyes gleam with challenge.

My lips curve up at that challenge because I *always* come out on top. "Here's what you get—I'll show up as your date for whatever excruciatingly awkward social situation next comes up on your calendar."

A glint of wickedness smolders in his eyes, bringing a low ache to my belly and a rush of heat to my entire body. I'm on a slippery slope here, fighting desire while negotiating with a man who never bends. "Ah, but you see, Paige, I don't have awkward social situations. No exes in my past who'd ever bother inviting me to anything."

I move to a quick defense. "Because you don't stick with anyone." It's not a question. He's a player. I mean, all the signs are there—he's a flirtatious, cocky man.

He shrugs one shoulder carelessly. "I can't help it if nothing lasts. Basic compatibility issue. Anyway, I don't hear anyone complaining."

"I bet your arrogance turns them off."

His eyes narrow. "I bet your bossiness turns guys away in droves."

Anger sparks through me. "You're the one who's bossy!"

"I am the boss. Of course I'm bossy."

I lift my chin. "I'm the boss too."

"Guess that keeps us both happily single. I enjoy the freedom."

"Me too," I say, forcing enthusiasm into my voice. The big 3-0 looms in my mind. Whatever. Age is just a number. Who cares if my younger sisters found their forever loves before me? That doesn't mean I'm doomed to be alone for the rest of my life. Right?

"The freer, the better," I add.

"Uh-huh." He gives me a knowing look that irks me. "So now that we've established I've got no future awkward social events on my calendar, what else can you offer?"

I swallow hard, flushed with heat and that low ache of desire that just won't quit. This is Spencer; obviously I'm not going there. I *can't* go there. One player in my life was plenty. "How about I use my real estate skills to help you find your first house? I'll forgo my commission to help you out." Before I was an innkeeper, I sold high-end real estate in Manhattan. Great pay, terrible stress, which is why I moved to Summerdale to run a B&B with my sister. Who knew I'd have so much stress here in the country too?

"How do you know I don't already have a house?" he asks, challenge in his voice.

"You're single and clearly need extra money, or you wouldn't be working a side gig as a caterer. I figure you're saving up for a decent place."

He scowls. "I'm saving to start a restaurant of my own."

"Oh, so where do you live currently? I could get you an upgrade."

His jaw clenches. "Why do you assume I live in a crappy place? I rent a nice house by the lake."

I exhale sharply. "I'm not trying to insult you. I'm trying to offer my expert real estate services."

"No offense, but I don't think there's anything you have to offer that I'd want."

And then he walks out the door.

My jaw hangs open. I can't believe he just walked out like that. Nothing to offer? I've got plenty to offer. I can sell real estate; I can stage a home for sale; I can run a frigging inn!

And I need to rub him in my ex's face!

"Wait!"

I race down the stairs after him, but he's gone. My shoulders slump. I need more chocolate. I should check the inn's pantry for any chocolate I missed. I sigh, running a hand through my hair. Maybe instead of self-soothing with chocolate and wine, I should finally get the dog I've been wanting. My sister's dog, Scout, is a bundle of unconditional love, which sounds pretty good about now.

No, a dog's a lot of work and might make a mess at the inn. That's on hold, just like my love life, until the inn gets better established.

I walk down the hallway, turn the corner, and slam into hard male chest. I jump back with a gasp of surprise and meet Spencer's gleaming eyes. My heart beats wildly.

He flashes a wolfish grin that brings every nerve ending to full attention. "Did you have something else to offer? I sense your revenge streak is stronger than your dislike of dealing with me."

"I don't mind dealing with you." *Much.* Then I take offense. "You know, whenever someone says 'no offense, but...' they always mean offense. So *I* should be the one who's insulted here. I have plenty to offer, you know."

"We can both be insulted. You implied I live in a crap place."

I huff. "I was trying to help you!"

He lifts his palms. "Hey, I was perfectly willing to help

you stick it to your ex, but you refuse to offer anything of value."

"What do you want?" I ask in exasperation.

His eyes meet mine intently for a moment. "It doesn't matter. Let's be real here. We'd never convince anyone we're a couple."

I deflate, my hopeful business opportunity and devastatingly fitting revenge fantasy vanishing. He's right. We can barely have a civil conversation. The fact that I *may* have felt a few flutters of desire for him only proves how long it's been since I've had anything resembling a love life. Still, some part of me can't let it go.

"But you're the only one arrogant enough to match Noah's oversized ego," I blurt.

He lets out an exaggerated sigh. "Fine. Give me a kiss. It'll only prove my point. No one would ever believe—"

I cut him off with a quick hard kiss that sends a shock of sensation through me. Our eyes meet up close, a new awareness simmering between us.

He eases back a step, staring at my lips before his gaze trails to my throat. I swallow. *Can he see the pulse point beating wildly there?*

He moves slowly with deliberate intent, closing the distance between us, his hand coming up to cradle my jaw. His head dips down, his lips hovering over mine for a heart-stopping moment. My breath quickens as my eyes close, my body humming in anticipation. Finally, his lips meet mine in a soft brush. Once, twice. Sweet and fiery pleasure shoots through me. And then he turns demanding, the kiss rough as his tongue thrusts inside. My world tilts on its axis. His large hand curves beneath my jaw, his arm banding around my waist, pulling me flush against him. Wrapped in his spicy scent and intoxicating heat, I couldn't move if I wanted to. *Bliss.*

When he finally lets me up for air, his eyes smolder into mine. "Well?"

I work on keeping my breathing even. "Terrible."

He smiles and releases his hold on me. "Liar. Looks like I've earned husband privileges."

My heart pounds hard, adrenaline racing through me. Husband privileges as in spending the night together? Of course he'd want something in return, but this? Why would he even go there? Well, we do have chemistry, that much is clear. Maybe he gets turned on by a woman who can give as good as she gets.

But he works for me, and I promised myself I'd wait for the right guy to come along who had potential for a serious relationship. How could I ever be serious about Spencer when we can't stop fighting?

His thumb brushes across my lower lip, clouding my mind with fresh desire. "Having second thoughts?"

I take a step back. "Well, yeah, I mean…it's a pretty big leap from where we were. Did you mean one night together or, like, an actual honeymoon of a week? Two weeks is out of the question."

His eyes widen and then gleam like a wolf closing in on its prey. His heated gaze trails from my eyes to my jaw and then lower to my throat. A hot shiver races through me.

His voice is husky. "I like where you're going with this. Let's keep it simple. One night. No strings."

And then while I stand there, trying to wrap my head around this unexpected condition to my plan, his lips meet mine. The kiss is gentle this time as he fits his lips over mine, one angle, then another, like he's exploring something new. He deepens the kiss, and my knees go weak, a low ache of desire making my limbs heavy. I clutch the front of his shirt to steady myself and keep him close.

Long moments later, he lifts his head, a question in his eyes.

*Yes. The answer is yes.* My stomach jumps at the thought.

"It's black tie," I manage to say.

He glances down at my fingers still clutching his shirt. My cheeks heat, but before I can pull away, he captures my wrists in a firm grip, one in each hand. He lifts my wrist and kisses the tender skin on the inside of one and then the other. I can barely breathe at the shockingly sweet gesture.

"I'll see you then, wife," he says.

"Bye," I whisper.

He swaggers away, full of arrogance like he won that round. I let out a shaky breath. I might be off balance and still in shock, but I'm not so sure I lost.

The next day my sister Brooke is back from her honeymoon with Max in Bermuda. She's positively glowing. She resembles me with brown hair and fair skin, except her eyes are green. Mine are a light brown. She used to be terribly jaded about men, even swore off them for a while using my old engagement ring to keep them away as her "anti-man shield." Ever since she got engaged to Max, the landscape designer we hired for the inn, she's been a ball of sunshine. Guess married life agrees with her.

Our guests checked out this morning, and we're having a lunch of salad fresh from our vegetable garden. We're in the dining area of the inn just off the kitchen. It's Tuesday, and we're not expecting more guests until Friday. It makes me nervous not to have a full guest list every day of the week. I know we're new, so I need to keep reasonable expectations. No wonder I'm still stressed out here in the country.

Brooke sets her fork down halfway through her salad. She shakes her head, her green eyes sparkling. "Listen to me going on and on about Bermuda. How was the holiday weekend here? I know it couldn't have been easy to handle a full inn alone. Of course, you did have Spencer here for part of it to help."

More like an aggravation than a help, and then something entirely unexpected, which I can't bring myself to share. After all the complaining I've done about Spencer, she'd probably laugh to hear I kissed him or agreed to go with him anywhere, let alone…

I press my lips together. "I wouldn't call him a help."

She spears a cherry tomato. "He took care of feeding guests on the Fourth of July. That's a help. Then you just had to direct them to the lake for fireworks."

My mind flashes to my agreement with Spencer. I RSVP'd yes to the wedding invitation last night, convincing myself there's a slew of reasons why it's a good idea—networking, revenge, kissing plus more with Spencer—but now, in the cold light of day, I'm having serious doubts.

Spencer's voice rings through my head. *Give me a kiss. It'll only prove my point. No one would ever believe—*

Then I rose to the challenge. Of course I did. I never back down from a challenge.

So what's one more challenge when there's so much upside for the inn by going to the wedding? Obviously I can't show up there alone. I let out a breath. I can handle Spencer. A flash of heat goes through me just thinking about handling that big muscular body. It was shockingly easy to forget our differences when we were kissing. *Focus!*

I take a sip of water. "So, uh, I have a wedding to go to the last Saturday of the month in the city. I probably won't be back until late Sunday. Can you cover for me?"

"Of course. Who's getting married?"

Spencer's husky voice echoes in my mind. *One night. No strings.*

Brooke knows Spencer rubs me the wrong way. And now I'm going to let him rub me the *right* way. I flush hot at the thought and take another drink of water. "A former client." Partially true, anyway. Noah was my client, which was how we met.

She cocks her head. "Wow, you're suddenly going to a lot of weddings. First Kayla's, then mine, this one in the city, and we have a wedding here this weekend. Spencer's still on for catering, right? I hope you didn't fight with him again. We're going to lose him if you keep it up."

My mouth goes dry just hearing his name. How awkward will it be to see him after our kiss?

After I agreed to a no-strings hookup?

That's not like me. Okay, fine, I can admit it, the kiss was scorching hot. Any woman would find it hard to turn down more of that kind of panty-melting passion. It doesn't come along every day, you know?

And look at the great revenge angle. Noah will see me in a new light. Instead of the fiancée he left behind, I'll be the successful business owner, happily married to her gorgeous five-star chef husband. I like the optics. Never mind what's supposed to happen afterward with my fake husband. A low ache of desire alarms me. He's not even here, and I'm excited just at the thought.

Shit. I can't do this. I *shouldn't* do this. I'm way too into the idea of a hookup, and there's no future with Spencer. Worse, he's on my payroll. The irony is I gave Brooke a hard time for hooking up with Max when he was on our payroll. I slipped into big-sister mode, lecturing her about not getting involved with someone working for you. I called her unprofessional. Of course, now they're happily married, but that would never happen with me and Spencer. We'd kill each other first.

"Paige? Did something happen with Spencer? Please tell me you didn't fire him."

"He's not fired. Don't worry."

She wipes pretend sweat from her forehead with the back of her hand and goes back to her lunch.

Fired. Ha. Quite the opposite. I hired him for double duty with my body as his payment. A bold move on his part. He must've been as turned on as I was by that kiss to suggest it. Maybe, deep down, he respects a strong woman, and it made him want more from me. Yeah, let's go with that.

I'm rationalizing again. Waffling back and forth because the idea of a night with him intrigues me. And I never would've said that before we kissed. Me, Paige Winters, the same woman who's had exactly two relationships in my thirty years and only a few groomsman flings in vulnerable moments that I like to pretend never happened.

That's how I'll handle this. Spencer will be like a groomsman fling—a much-needed release after the emotional upheaval of the wedding. Then I'll promptly file that fling in the never-happened category.

I rub the side of my neck, remembering our kiss. The smoldering heat and hardness of his body pressed against mine, his lips gentle and then rough, taking as he pleased. The sweet fiery pleasure.

I'm not sure I'll be able to forget a night with him.

## 3

I walk into the Summerdale library that night for my first book club meeting. I saw a notice about it in the *Summerdale Sheet*, the online weekly newspaper I recently started reading. It's important as a local business owner to stay current with the latest goings-on. That's how I knew about the fireworks at the lake, the opening of a chapter of Best Friends Care at the animal shelter, and ladies' night at The Horseman Inn.

Best Friends Care trains shelter dogs to be therapy companions for veterans with PTSD, a worthy cause. Famous actress Harper Ellis, who grew up in Summerdale, is heavily involved with the charity and was the driving force behind setting up the program. I was surprised to hear about ladies' night, which apparently my own sister Kayla and sister-in-law Sydney attend every week and never bothered to tell me about. Hmph. I'm good company. Granted, I've been working a lot, but it's important I network locally. I'll be there this Thursday night.

Today's book club meeting is not about networking. It's just for me. I love reading and discussing stories with like-minded people. Audrey, the librarian who runs the group, has good taste in books. I looked up the previous reads on the library's website.

I wave to her as she approaches from a back room, her

hands full with two grocery bags. She's a petite brunette with a reserved disposition. Kayla says Audrey's slow to warm up, but once she does, you're in.

"Hi, Paige," Audrey says, giving me a sweet smile. "So glad you could make it. We'll be setting up over here." She jerks her head toward a group of cushioned chairs around a circular wooden table over by the New Books section.

I hurry over to her and reach for a bag. "Here, let me help you with that."

She hands it over with a quick thanks.

I peek inside—Wheat Thins, cheese, and olives, as well as plastic cups.

She sets her bag on the table and starts dragging the cushioned armchairs with a wooden base into a circle around the table. I help her. The chairs are heavy, and we have to push them across the gray speckled carpet.

She adjusts a chair to be more equidistant between two other chairs. "Please tell me you read *Goddess of the Rivers*."

"Of course. I want to be part of the discussion."

She studies the circle of chairs critically and then makes one final adjustment. "You'd be surprised how many people just come to gossip and eat snacks."

"Good evening, Audrey," an older man calls.

We both turn to where three elderly men and two elderly women just arrived at the entrance. A white shuttle bus drives away behind them. They must've gotten a ride on a senior citizen shuttle. Audrey and I are the youngest ones here by at least four decades.

"I know, I know," she says quietly as they shuffle in, talking loudly amongst themselves. "I've been trying to recruit some younger people. I had three moms in their forties for a while but lost them when things got busy with their kids' sports schedules. Sloane should be here tonight though. Have you met her? She's around our age. She's on that car show on the Turbo Channel and also fixes cars at Murray's." She stares at the ceiling. "What's it called?" She snaps her fingers. "*The Right Fix*. I only watched it once. Cars aren't my thing."

"Cool. I met her briefly. She was at Kayla's wedding."

"You'll like her, though she's not great about finishing the book."

She gestures for everyone to take their seats. It takes a while because one of the men really wants to sit between the two older women, and they don't want him there. I stifle a laugh. Audrey and I take chairs next to each other and wait.

My eye catches on a few magazines fanned out on the table. The glossy women's magazine on top says in bold letters: 5 Signs You're Falling for a Player. My gut does a slow roll. I know the signs. It happened with Noah. *Crap.* I can't let that happen again with Spencer. I don't care how much lust I felt during that kiss. The man flirts shamelessly with every woman who crosses his path. I can't risk it.

Finally, after everyone's settled, Audrey says, "Hello, everyone. I brought a new bookworm, Paige Winters."

Everyone claps, and my throat tightens. Seems silly to get so emotional, but I don't get much applause just for showing up. Not even after I bust my ass to get a job done right. When you're a hard worker who achieves results, people come to expect it of you.

I smile. "Thanks for the warm welcome, everyone."

Audrey introduces the rest of the group to me as Mr. or Mrs., out of respect for their age. After that, there's a lot of talk about the food as Audrey sets everything out.

"You outdid yourself this week," Mr. Paulson says, grabbing a handful of Wheat Thins.

"Just the usual stuff," Audrey says. "Though I did find a nice gouda cheese. Give that a try if cheese agrees with you."

This sets off an animated discussion on what foods agree or don't agree with them. Audrey and I exchange a smile.

Sloane arrives, and Audrey removes her stuff from the seat she reserved next to her. "Thanks for holding my spot," Sloane says. "Hi, everyone. I didn't get to finish the book, but the beginning was good." She glances over at me. "Oh, hey. Kayla's sister, right? Paige."

"That's right. Nice to see you again."

Audrey smiles. "Everyone's here, so let's get started."

It's kind of a strange book club. Audrey first tries to open the discussion to thoughts on the book. I'm the only one with something specific to say. A few general comments of the "I liked it" variety follow. Then Audrey falls back on book club discussion questions. Unfortunately, once it becomes clear I'm the only one willing to respond to her questions, probably because I'm the only one who read the book, Audrey gives up and lets everyone chat and eat, which is probably why they're here. Senior citizen *fiesta*.

After the meeting ends, Sloane dashes off, saying over her shoulder, "I've got to take Huckleberry out. Caleb's away for work."

Sloane is engaged to Caleb Robinson. He's my sister-in-law Sydney's youngest brother. I guess that makes us all family. I should spend more time getting to know the various Robinsons. They're one of the founding families here in Summerdale.

I help Audrey clean up and say under my breath, "You made a valiant effort."

The seniors are slowly getting up from their chairs, still talking animatedly about everything but the book.

She nods and heads to a back room behind the circulation desk. I follow her. We throw out the garbage and put the leftover food in the staff refrigerator.

She turns to me. "If I could be pickier and say only show up if you're willing to read the book, I would, but I'm afraid it would just be me sitting here. Once in a while another person reads it, which makes it not a complete bust. It's random who reads the book week to week."

"Maybe a monthly meeting would work out better than every other week. That would give people more time to read."

"I guess. I read so much in a week, it's hard for me to remember some people can actually put a book down to do other things."

I laugh and follow her back out to the main area of the library. We say goodbye to the other book club members.

Every single one thanks her profusely on their way out. The shuttle bus is idling right outside the entrance.

After they leave, she says, "You want to get a drink and talk about the book?"

I blink, surprised. "Like a book club after the book club?"

"Yes. The unofficial meeting for those who officially read it."

I smile. "Sure."

"Great! I'll just lock up here and meet you over at The Horseman."

∾

A short time later, I'm seated at the bar of The Horseman Inn with Audrey. It's a Tuesday night, and we're the only two at the bar. A few people are eating in the front dining room. We're both nursing a glass of pinot grigio while we take a deep dive into *Goddess of the Rivers*.

"It's a masterpiece," I conclude. "History, politics, layer upon layer building the emergence of an incredibly strong woman."

"Yes, yes, yes!" she exclaims, grabbing my arm. "You get it. Paige, where have you been hiding? Please tell me you'll be at book club from now on."

I smile. "The official senior citizen version or this one at the bar?"

"Both! I still hold out hope that more people will join us." She takes a sip of wine. "If you can believe this, I started the book club with the secret hope I might meet a single guy there who loves reading. It's on my short list for a relationship."

*She has a list?*

"What else is on the short list?"

She lifts one shoulder. "Good manners. Just two things. What can I say, my expectations have shrunk after an incredibly unsuccessful attempt at online dating. Can I be frank?"

I gesture her on. "Please do."

"I'm thirty."

"'Nuf said. I know the big 3-0 crisis. Just went through it on my birthday three days ago." I take a healthy swallow of wine. "Still going through it."

"So you get it. My best friends are married now. Well, you know Sydney, she's pregnant. It won't be long until Jenna is too."

"And Kayla's married now, though she says she's waiting for kids."

Audrey sighs. "Sloane's engaged too. I'm like the third wheel to absolutely everyone. And the irony is, I was the only one who wanted a serious relationship all along. Sydney fought like cats and dogs with Wyatt for months. She called him Satan."

I laugh. "Still does, though now it's meant affectionately."

She inclines her head. "Jenna never wanted a relationship; now she's married to Eli. Kayla swore she was just friends with Adam and then boom! Married. And Sloane was shocked that Caleb pursued her. She didn't have to make any effort whatsoever. Meanwhile, I'm scrolling through dating profile after dating profile and suffering through first dates, and I do mean suffering."

I give her arm a squeeze in sympathy. "No question it's rough out there."

"Right? I've been looking forward to a husband and kids for years, yet here I am the only single one left." She finishes her wine and signals the bartender, Betsy, for another drink. She turns to me. "Can I get you another one?"

"Sure, why not?"

"I can walk home from here. Hey, you can crash at my place if you're not good to drive."

"I'll keep that in mind, thanks, though I've got a pretty good tolerance for alcohol."

"Then we're good to go. So what's your story? Are your sisters treating you like the third wheel while they talk all things wedding and honeymoon and brag about their husbands? No offense to your sisters. In my experience, all newlyweds brag about this stuff."

Our fresh glasses of wine arrive, and she clinks her glass against mine in a toast. "To third wheels."

I smile. "My sisters are giddy in love and can't help but talk about that stuff. The good news is you and I can be the third and fourth wheel, so it's all balanced again."

She gives me a sympathetic look. "So you do feel like the odd one out."

I run a finger down the stem of my glass, thinking about that. "I'm happy for them, and it's not like I'm jealous. I wouldn't marry either of those guys." *Not my type.* Which is exactly what I said about Spencer, and then he was kissing me, and suddenly we fit. *No, no, no. Not going there.*

She giggles. "Say how you really feel."

We take a sip of wine, sharing a secret smile with our eyes.

I lower my voice. "Adam barely speaks, and Max is too laid-back, even his hair is laid-back, all ruffled every which way. I need someone more my speed."

"What's your speed? Fast?" She slaps a hand over her mouth. "I didn't mean that as dirty as it came out. Though who'd want a fast guy in bed?"

I giggle, which is so unlike me. I think the wine is going to my head. "I'm driven. I set a goal and don't stop until I reach it. Then I set the next bigger goal."

"So you're looking for a type A overachiever like yourself."

"Not an overachiever just...an achiever. A guy who's ambitious, who has goals and makes things happen."

"Your short list is much shorter than mine, and I hate to say it, Paige, but guys like that are in short supply around here. You'd have better luck in a corporate boardroom in the city, you know?"

I shake my head. "Probably right. If I'd stayed in banking, I'd most likely be married to another banker, living in the burbs with two point three kids and a dog by now."

She tosses back her wine. "A dog is very important for the family picture. I can't have a dog because I have a cat, and she would not be happy with that. Anyway, what were we talking about?"

"Our short lists?"

"God, I'm so sick of hoping, you know? I'm just going to give up on the wife/mom fantasy and throw myself into my work."

"Is it, uh, busy at the library?" It seems a small quiet place.

"The children's room gets very busy with all of our programs. I love kids." She gets a wistful look on her face. "Do you love kids?"

"I haven't had much experience with them." I think about the messy, misbehaving kids at the inn. "I guess some of them could be okay."

She leans close, smiling. "Can I tell you a secret?"

I turn to her in surprise. I don't know her well, and while we have the single-at-thirty thing in common and similar tastes in books, I'm not sure she should be spilling secrets to me. Though I'm extremely curious what a reserved librarian could possibly have a secret about. Did she decide to have a baby on her own since she loves kids so much? Or maybe she has a friends-with-benefits situation she hasn't told anyone about. That seems more likely from a reserved thinker like herself.

"Okay," I say. "I won't tell a soul. Is it about a guy?"

She shakes her head. "I'm going to write the next Great American Novel. That's the work I'm going to dedicate myself to tirelessly. I've already started. I get up at five a.m. every day to work on it before my day job. I do another hour after dinner and spend as much time as I can on the week-ends. I haven't told anyone because it's my super-secret project. It makes me feel good to have my own special thing."

"Wow. That's great. What's it about?"

"I can't tell you that. But I've got fifty pages of what will be an epic family saga."

"Very cool."

"Now you tell me a secret."

I look into her kind blue eyes and find myself confiding, "I'm considering going to a wedding with a guy, who will remain nameless, as my fake husband, and in return for this favor, he wants me to spend one night with him."

"Get out!"

"Shh!"

"Paige, do you *want* to spend the night with this guy?"

I glance around, suddenly conscious of the fact that Spencer is the chef here. He could be in the kitchen as we speak. "Forget I said anything."

"I can't do that. Kayla always describes you as tough as nails. Why would you agree to something you don't want to do?"

I rub the back of my neck, ducking my head. How can I explain my Spencer wedding revenge plan and the lust that caught me off guard? I don't want to sound like a sad rejected woman who keeps lusting for players. Ugh. What is wrong with me?

Audrey ducks her head to meet my eyes. "I swear you can trust me with whatever's going on. Doesn't leave this room."

I believe her, so I share part of it, about my ex inviting me to his wedding to the woman he cheated on me with and how the invitation arrived on my thirtieth birthday.

Audrey immediately comes to my defense. "Well, of course you had a lapse of judgment. That's a three-oh apocalypse. I'll go as your plus-one. Don't give this one- night-guy another thought. At our age, we're not looking for a fling and certainly not one being forced on us."

"I wouldn't say forced." I lift one shoulder in a careless shrug. "It's not like I haven't had a wedding fling before. I mean, how many times can I be a bridesmaid and not get a major case of FOMO and grab on to my assigned partner in a tux?"

"So you're cool with it?"

My mind flashes to Spencer and his arrogance. The way he swaggered off like he won that round.

"He took advantage of my one-third life crisis," I declare. "I'm going to call it off right now." I stand.

"Does that mean I'm your plus-one?"

"Yes. Thank you. The wedding is a major networking opportunity for the inn. I'll explain later." I look toward the staff door I've seen Sydney go through many times. "I'll be right back." I head toward the door.

"I know who it is!" she exclaims.

I ignore that and march resolutely into a kitchen with two guys who look to be in their thirties cooking at burners and one guy chopping carrots. I hadn't considered the kitchen would be busy. There are only a few customers in the dining room.

My gaze zeroes in on the broad back of Spencer in a white chef jacket, black trousers, and black sneakers. "Excuse me," I say.

All four men turn toward me in surprise.

One corner of Spencer's mouth curves up, bringing a rush of heat. "Paige Winters in my kitchen. Miss me?"

# 4

I steel myself against his obvious charms. "No."

The other guys in the kitchen chuckle. I glare at them before fixing my gaze on Spencer. It's time I put him in his place. "Can you take a short break?"

He jerks his chin at me and instructs one of the guys on what needs to be done. Then he steps out the back door into the dark of night.

Guess I'm supposed to follow him out there, huh?

I take a deep bracing breath and step through the doorway outside just as he flips on an overhead light. It gives off a soft yellow glow that makes the angles of his face look sharper, more masculine and hard.

I cross my arms, looking for the righteous feeling I had earlier when I was with Audrey. "I don't need you as my revenge date for my ex's wedding anymore. I found someone else."

"That so?"

I nod vigorously, making myself dizzy. I might've had too much wine. "Yeah, so you can forget that whole one-night-together thing you wanted."

He reaches out and tucks a lock of hair behind my ear. My breath stutters out. His gaze smolders into mine for a timeless moment. My heart pounds, my breath quickening.

He dips his head, leaning in. Closer, closer still. My body hums in anticipation. The man takes his time, dragging things out in the most tantalizing way.

His words run hot over my lips. "Paige, honey."

*Honey. That's nice.* "Yes?"

"You're the one who suggested a night together." He pulls back to look at me. "Or was it a week in my bed?"

I blink a few times, trying to process this blatantly false statement. "No, you said you earned husband privileges."

"The privilege of being your fake husband *as a wedding date.*"

I stare at him as my mind flashes back to that conversation. How could I have been so far off?

He brushes the back of his fingers down the cord of my neck, sparking fire over my skin. I swallow hard, telling myself to ignore the desire he so easily stokes. He's toying with me.

His voice turns husky. "I realized you must've liked that kiss enough to explore more, so I went along, see where it leads."

"But you said one night, no strings!"

"After you said a night or a week. I chose a night to keep things simple." He sounds entirely too reasonable and not at all worked up about our potential hookup.

I fight back a blush and lose. All this time I was agonizing over what I thought was his condition, alternately wanting and rejecting the idea, while he was just going along for the ride to see how much he could get from me. Of course he'd prefer one night. Player alert!

I purse my lips. "You were just being a guy."

He clutches both hands to his heart, staggering back. "Ooh, low blow. I'm in guy territory." He gets serious. "So who're you going with?"

"Audrey."

He smirks. "Audrey." He puts a hand down to his chest level. "Petite brunette, runs the library?"

I bristle. "Yes. What's wrong with that? She offered."

He leans close, sending another wave of heat through my entire body. "How's that going to show up your ex?"

I square my shoulders and straighten my spine. "In case you forgot, I'm mostly going to this wedding to pitch the inn to the best man's travel magazine and network with some very influential people."

"Uh-huh, and to stick it to your ex that you're now a happily married woman. That's why you needed the Spencer ammunition. Didn't you say I'm the only one who could match his big ego? Let's not forget your lust for me."

I lift my chin. "Audrey will be a perfectly acceptable replacement for you."

His eyes light up. "You're going as a couple. Brilliant move!"

"She's going more as support," I mutter.

"What's that?" he asks cheerfully.

I scowl. He was supposed to be *devastated* that he has no chance of sleeping with me. Now he's turned it all around like it was my idea. He's perfectly fine with my rejection. So unfair. He was the one who was supposed to be obsessing about our night together after the wedding. Not that I was ever obsessing.

"Well, good night." I turn on my heel and grab the handle of the back door, pulling it. The damn thing doesn't budge. "Did you lock us out here?" I exclaim.

His hand reaches past me, the heat of his chest close to my back. His deep voice rumbles by my ear, making me nearly dizzy with lust. "So quick to suspect me of wrongdoing." It's the wine effect making me dizzy, I assure myself. Not him. "It gets stuck sometimes in the heat." He gives the handle a tug, and it pops open.

I dash inside, face flushed. His coworkers are grinning. I bet he takes lots of women out back for private time. I'm so glad I cut things off before they went any further.

"See you Saturday," he calls.

I stiffen. Crap. I forgot we have a wedding at the inn this Saturday, and he's catering. I'll make Brooke deal with him. I hurry out, escaping to Audrey's company.

As soon as I sit down, she says, "Smart move. Spencer flirts with everyone and doesn't take any woman seriously. It was Spencer who was going to be your fake-husband wedding date with a bonus, right? He's the only single one of the kitchen crew."

I'm so overheated I'm tempted to fan myself, but I resist in the name of dignity. "Yes. He's such an ass."

She nudges my shoulder with hers. "You and me, Paige. We'll do great things. I'm going to write my novel and finally travel the country—on my book tour, of course—and you're going to…" She looks at me expectantly.

I press my lips together, determined to do something great just like her. "I'm going to put my inn on the map. It will be the *destination*, not just a stop on the way to somewhere else."

She lifts her glass to me. "Ya see, that's the nice thing about being a mature single woman. You can pour all your energy into a worthy cause. To goals! And achievers like you."

I clink my glass against hers. "And achievers like you too. Who needs men?"

She doesn't drink to that because just then Sydney's oldest brother, Drew, swaggers on by. We're kinda family through marriage. Even though he let his dark brown hair grow on the shaggy side and sports scruff on his jaw, he still has the sharp fit look of a soldier. He's a former Army Ranger and now runs a dojo in town. Guess being a black belt helps keep him looking lethal. If I didn't know him through family, I'd find him slightly scary. But, in a way, he's like my brother, Wyatt— protective of his younger siblings. Sydney says Drew always looked out for the four of them, especially after their mom died too soon.

"Hey, Drew," I say.

His gaze is locked on Audrey, but he spares me a quick glance. "Hey."

Audrey's cheeks pinken under his steady gaze. Her fingers flutter in the air. "Enjoy your game."

His lips curve into a hint of a smile. "Enjoy your pinot

grigio." He continues on his way to a corner table to watch the Yankees game on the TV mounted above the bar.

"I will!" she calls to him in a belligerent tone. As comebacks go, it was a bit late and strangely hostile.

He jerks his chin at her and goes back to the game.

She huffs.

"Are you okay?" I ask her.

She leans forward, yelling across the bar, "It's not wrong to have a favorite!"

He stares at her intently.

She lifts her chin. "Once I like something, I always like it."

A slow sexy smile takes him from slightly scary to panty-melting. Even I feel it across the room. Audrey's lips part, her color high.

There's something going on here, some subtext I'm missing.

She grabs her wine and takes a small sip, a pleasant expression pasted on her face like she's proving that she really likes pinot grigio.

"How did he know what we're drinking?" I ask her.

She startles, setting her glass down with a clatter. "Huh? What?"

"I said, how did he know what we're drinking?"

She keeps her voice low. "He knows what I drink because he says I'm predictable. Translation: boring."

"Rude."

"Yeah."

I lean close and whisper, "Still, that smile he gave you looked like there might be something between you. Or potential?"

She whispers back, "He only smiled because he was remembering how I used to have a crush on him when I was a teenager. He's teasing like I still like him."

"Do you?"

"I'm over it."

"Maybe he feels the same way. Maybe he was coming on to you."

She scoffs. "No. I know for sure that's not it, which is fine because I'm over it. Him. I'm over him."

"How are you so sure he's not into you?"

She presses her lips together. "I don't want to talk about it."

"Okay."

She whispers fiercely, "It's embarrassing enough I used to write to him like I was writing in my diary when he was away on military deployments. Gushing emails full of exclamation points and emojis. Imagine a teen me sending daily emails to my unrequited crush, a Special Forces soldier in a war zone."

I cringe. Thank God there's no evidence from my own unrequited teenaged crush. He was three years older and didn't know I existed.

She shakes her head, staring at the bar, her voice barely audible. "I can never live it down. My only consolation is that I'm sure after all these years he doesn't have those emails to throw in my face."

"Oh, I don't think he'd do that." I try to put a positive spin on it to lessen her embarrassment. "It probably cheered him up to hear from you."

She downs her wine, sneaking a look over at him. I take a peek too. He appears to be engrossed in the game. He didn't order a drink or food. Doesn't he have a TV at his place?

Audrey's face and neck are flushed pink. I'm dying to know why she's so sure he's not into her, but she said she didn't want to talk about it, and I don't know her well enough to push.

"You still like him though, right?" I ask. "He seems like a good guy."

"We're friends," she says evenly. "He asked if we could be friends, and I agreed."

"Really?" *Ooh, the friend zone. No wonder she's pissy.*

"Yeah, we kinda grew up together since I'm close with Sydney, we live in the same town—"

"Okay, you can totally tell me to shut up, but it seems to me the best way to erase the embarrassing memories is to replace them with new cooler Audrey moments. If you're really friends, then why not let him get to know you now? You could tell him about your book."

"Shut up."

"That's fair." I lift my glass. "The hell with men." Spencer's smoldering gaze flashes through my mind, and I ruthlessly push the memory away.

"Right," Audrey says softly, her gaze lingering over my shoulder.

I turn to see the scruffy profile of a man whose sole focus is on the game. Or is it?

## 5

*Spencer*

I'm not chasing after Paige. Chasing is for desperate guys, which I am *not*.

I've thought long and hard about it, and Audrey just won't be a good substitute as Paige's plus-one in this particular situation. And it's not about any kind of touchy-feely thing for Paige. I'm honor bound to step in. Hey, I saw her cry face over her ex, and her sister Kayla spilled all the dirty details to me. Kayla used to waitress at The Horseman Inn where I work. (A really bad waitress too, but so adorably cheerful about her mistakes no one minded.)

Anyway, Kayla is a classic oversharer and told me Paige's ex, Noah, was an arrogant womanizer who Paige believed was simply admirably confident. She was convinced he'd reformed his womanizing ways when he fell in love with her, as evidenced by his proposal. News flash—people don't change. Clearly I need to avenge her honor. She's been wronged, and I can make things right.

I'm catering again for a Saturday elopement wedding at the inn. I'm in the kitchen, keeping an eye on Paige on the patio, just waiting for my moment. The sun hits her wavy brown hair, bringing out highlights that remind me of caramel. Brooke's supposedly in charge today, but Paige can't resist checking on the wedding proceedings. Always the boss, that one. Guess it goes along with being the older sister. I'm an only child.

She shifts in her floral V-neck blouse and tight navy pants, her curvy figure making the blood rush through my veins. She glances over her shoulder toward the kitchen window, and I quickly busy myself tossing a caprese salad. What am I waiting for? I should just go out there and tell her how it's going to be. Audrey is *not* going to be the serious artillery Paige needs for the situation she's found herself in. Paige has to think strategically and obliterate the competition. I can make her ex regret losing her. Given the chance, I can unleash major payback.

Brooke dashes inside, surprising me. I was too focused on her sister to notice her approach. Her dark hair is up in a bun, her cheeks flushed pink. "Hi! We're about to start in five minutes. Just wanted to check how it's going in here. Menu good?"

"All's well. The cherries looked good this morning, so I added cherry tarts to the dessert menu, along with the coconut wedding cake."

She beams a smile. "Awesome! Can't wait to try some. I'm going to let the bride know we're good to go."

I nod and get back to work. Brooke is almost as sweet as Kayla. Don't know where Paige was when the sweet genes were passed out in that family. Of course, her older brother, Wyatt, isn't sweet. More like a gruff know-it-all, but hey, he's earned it. Tech billionaire by his twenties. He must know his shit.

What is it about Paige that gets under my skin? Half the time I want to throttle her. I try not to think about what I want to do the other half of the time. Not professional. She's a valued client. So what if I kissed her? I was just proving my point, that no one would believe us as a couple. And then that kiss—fire. Now it's become this constant nagging in my mind to do something about it. Follow up on that fire.

My wiser self says not to get involved. Let's be honest—

after the initial lust passed, we'd go right back to our battle stations.

I never thought she'd suggest a night together. In the heat of the moment, I agreed, and now that it's off the table, I want it even more.

No, I need to rise above my baser needs and do my duty. Paige needs me.

I check in with my two assistants, who're preparing mini quiches for appetizers. Then I get to work on shrimp puffs. Catering here for elopements and inner-circle weddings is a pretty easy gig. Mostly appetizers, salads, and desserts. There's no crowd to feed. Everyone just wants to graze, dance, and be merry.

Brooke hustles through with the young redheaded bride in a simple white cotton dress with embroidered white flowers. She's wearing a ring of flowers on her head with a trailing sheer veil. There's something nice about the simplicity of her outfit. The outdoor wedding under a pergola of white flowers too. Romantic. Not a word I've ever uttered in my life, but I can see how it fits.

The bride slowly heads toward her groom standing at the wooden pergola in the distance. I step outside to the deck and make my way down the steps to the patio, where Paige is supervising from a distance. Time to roll out the Wolf charm. Paige is so engrossed in the wedding she doesn't notice me approach.

I speak in a low voice near her ear. "Hello, future wife."

She jumps, her hand covering her heart. "You scared me," she hisses.

I bite back a smile and remain focused on charming her. "I know you were scared. You got cold feet over our marriage."

Her brows knit together over light brown eyes. Whisky eyes. "Are you high?"

"I've thought it over, and I think the cure is to just do it."

"What the hell are you talking about?"

*Time for the big guns.* "You need me to make Noah regret ever letting you go. Audrey won't cut it." I pull a gold band from my pocket. That's right. I came prepared for our fake marriage.

Her jaw drops.

I take her hand and listen for the real wedding vows happening right now. Then I whisper along. "Paige Winters, will you promise to love and cherish Spencer Wolf for the rest of our fake married life?"

She blinks a few times and stares at my hand holding hers. Finally, her eyes meet mine, softer than usual. "What's the catch?"

"No catch. You'll simply owe me a favor to be collected later. In the meantime, I'll show Noah you're the wife of my dreams."

"Yes," she says in a breathy voice. "Let's do this."

I slide the gold band on her finger and give her the other band to give to me.

She glances at the wedding, which has moved on to really long vows the bride wrote herself. She's holding multiple pages of paper. Bad groom for going the uninspired route with the mayor's simple vow.

Paige dives in with her own version. "Spencer Wolf, will you promise to stay true to Paige Winters and never leave my side through the entire wedding and reception and be the perfect doting fake husband?"

"I do." A tickling of unease runs down my spine. I have never said those two words in a vow in my life, and it feels oddly like an authentic commitment. Ironic because I've never had a relationship that lasted more than a month.

She slides the ring on my finger and smiles. My heart thumps a little harder. That smile makes her look nearly angelic, more like the kind of woman I usually go for.

She admires the gold band on her finger and looks up at me, a new appreciation in her eyes. "Audrey's going to be disappointed. She liked the fake pregnancy idea you mentioned and wanted to be the pregnant one."

"Audrey won't bring the heat, though it's nice that she wants to help. You don't need nice on this occasion. You need me."

Paige holds out her hand, tilting it back and forth so the gold band catches the sunlight. "Where'd you get these? They look like real gold rings."

*Uh, the jewelry store. What a question.*

"Where do you usually get gold wedding bands? I dug up a couple of old graves and pulled them off two rotting corpses."

Her eyes dance with amusement. "For me?"

I bite back a laugh. "Of course."

"I can't believe you're all in like this after—"

I cut her off before she can remind me how much we normally battle. I'm trying to do the honorable thing here. "What was I supposed to do, let you walk into that wedding like a lamb to the slaughter? I saw your cry face."

She goes up on tiptoe and kisses my cheek just above my trimmed beard, where I can feel her warmth. It tingles on the spot. "Who would've guessed you'd turn out to be Prince Charming?"

I hook a finger in the buckle of her pants, tugging her closer. "Hang onto that thought when I collect on my favor."

Her eyes sparkle with secret glee. "I already know what I'm going to do for you."

My mind immediately flashes to dirty ideas. Before I can settle on my favorite, she continues.

"It's a surprise, but I think you'll like it. I'm starting to understand what motivates you."

"World domination?"

She gives me a wry look. "I understand ambition. I'm the same way."

The bride lets out a happy sound, throws her arms around her groom, and they kiss passionately. Brooke claps nearby, along with Mayor Levi Appleton. He's a single guy around my age, longish dark hair with a beard, wearing a dark gray suit. They must be paying him well. I don't know how else he can get through officiating all these boring weddings. *Vow, vow, kiss the bride, blah, blah, blah.* Call me a romantic.

I watch as Paige walks over to join them, her hips swaying in tight pants. Damn, I should've held out for a honeymoon.

∼

*Paige*

Three weeks later, I've managed not to fight with Spencer by keeping our conversations short and to the point. Even Brooke noticed how civil we've been with each other. Have my nerves ramped up with each passing day? Yes.

Has he gotten a decidedly lusty look in his eyes every time we see each other? I think so.

I suspect he's imagining our proposed one-night-only honeymoon, which I swear was his idea not mine. Anyway, I haven't given it another thought. Really. I have much more important things on my mind for my ex's wedding, like networking on behalf of the inn and showing Noah I'm doing better without him in my life.

I explained the change in plans to Audrey, and she was supportive of my decision to go with Spencer but a little worried because, well, he's not the relationship type. She didn't want me to get sucked in by his charms at a wedding, which can always make a single woman who's been a bridesmaid too many times vulnerable to poor decisions. Exhibit A: my past flings with groomsmen.

And, of course, my emotions will be running high. I know, I know, it's got all the makings of a disaster, but if I play it *just right*, it could be such a win for the inn. Eyes on the prize.

Today's the day. I've barely eaten in two days, but boy, have I gotten my beauty rest. I made sure to go to bed an hour earlier every night this week and took a power nap every afternoon. I'm going for the fresh dewy-eyed look of the youth I wasted on Noah. Now I'm thirty and have to work at it. At least I did today.

I spent hours getting ready, even going to the salon to get my hair freshly styled. Makeup is done perfectly. I'm wearing a new little black dress with a sexy bare back and strappy heels, gold wedding band in place. Can I really pull off being Spencer's wife? *Ahh!*

I pace my apartment. *This is a performance. You're confident, successful, and happily married. This wedding doesn't affect you in the least. You're there to show everyone that, especially Noah.*

I stop and let out a shaky breath. The financial pressures as a new inn owner are never far from my mind. This is a golden opportunity to fill the inn with guests fast. Influential people will be at this wedding, as well as the owner of a major media company. Summer is my last best shot to get the inn into the black.

My phone vibrates with a text.

Spencer: *I'm here. Let's get this show on the road.*

Right. *Show.* I take one last look in the mirror and hurry out the door. See, this isn't even a real date. If it were, Spencer would've made the short trek to knock on the inn's door. Instead, he waited in the car. My older brother, Wyatt, always used to say, if a guy's into you, they'll make an effort.

I take my time walking downstairs, working on keeping my breath nice and even. Not that I take Wyatt's advice to heart all the time, but he's usually right about guy speak, which is more about their actions than their words.

I step outside, and my breath stutters out.

Spencer is in a black tux, leaning against a silver stretch limousine. There's a bouquet of red roses in his hand.

I blink rapidly, hardly believing my eyes. My pulse skitters.

He straightens, giving me a sexy smile. "You look beautiful, wife."

I close the distance, breathless and a little dizzy over this unexpected event. I can't seem to find my voice. He hands me the flowers and kisses my cheek, warming it at the spot.

"Thank you," I manage. *Someone is finally taking the time to romance me!* And it's Spencer, my aggravating chef. I never would've guessed he had it in him.

He opens the back limo door for me.

"This is such a surprise." Understatement. I'm knocked on my ass with no sure footing.

He tips my chin up, gazing into my eyes. "Of course I'd go all out for my new wife. We're still in the honeymoon phase, beautiful, and I'm the luckiest man alive."

I impulsively hug him, my eyes hot. Then I get into the back seat, where champagne is chilling. I glance toward the driver to say hello, but the divider glass is closed, and I can only see the shadow of a man with short clipped hair. Soft jazz music plays.

Spencer joins me a moment later, his large frame seeming to take all the air out of the space.

I turn to him. "Thank you. I think I'm in shock."

One corner of his mouth curves up. "This way we can relax, drink if we feel like it, and not worry about driving. Besides, it'll give us time to get our stories straight."

The limo pulls out into the street, and my journey as Spencer's fake wife begins.

"Champagne?" he asks.

I'm going to enjoy this a lot more than I thought.

By the time the limo arrives at the church in midtown, I'm in Spencer's lap, giddy from champagne, and running my fingers along his short beard. He grew it at my request, and it's *sooo* sexy.

He tucks a lock of hair behind my ear. "It's good that you're comfortable touching me. More convincing for a married couple."

Somehow he doesn't seem affected by the champagne like I am. He sounds like his normal self, not super happy like me. His voice is a tad huskier, but I don't think champagne has that effect, or I would sound husky too. Why was I so worried about today? This will be easy.

"You should call me Paige," I whisper just in case the driver can hear our secret scheming. "Don't say wife because that sounds too formal. People might not believe it."

"Our gold bands will tell them all they need to know. Remember, we met at your successful inn, where I was a consultant for your breakfast menu—"

"Which you were!"

"And then we had dinner at my successful restaurant and

have been close ever since. We were together for how long before we got married?"

"Hmmm…not so long. We got married three weeks ago, which is funny because that is *exactly* when we exchanged those fake marriage vows."

"Which is why I chose that date. How long were we seeing each other before that?"

"I didn't know there'd be a pop quiz." I bite my lip, trying to remember. "It must've been this year since I just bought the farmhouse in January that became the inn."

He pinches my chin, directing my gaze to his. His blue eyes remind me of the sky on a summer day. "April. So we've been together four months total, three weeks of that happily married. We're waiting on the honeymoon until after your inn's busy summer season. Then we'll take a culinary tour of Europe."

I smile. "Because you're a chef. And because we love each other so much."

He kisses me, a tender kiss that feels real, like maybe he does love me. Warmth floods me as I gaze into his sky-blue eyes. This fake relationship feels so real, so intimate. A warning goes off in my mind. I have to remember we're pretending today. It's just that Spencer is an unexpectedly fantastic actor.

I run my fingers through the short hair at the nape of his neck. "Hard to believe you once thought no one would believe us as a couple."

"Mmm," he says noncommittally.

"One kiss opened the door—" I shut my mouth abruptly as the back door opens, surprising me. Our driver stands on the sidewalk, waiting for us. We've been sitting back here too long.

I clamber out awkwardly from Spencer's lap, my dress hitching up my hips with my effort. I stand on the sidewalk, smoothing out my little black dress while Spencer gives the driver instructions for the reception at a hotel a few blocks away.

The driver nods and walks back to the driver's side, setting off to park somewhere.

Spencer crooks his elbow for me, and I take it, suddenly light-headed. Is it nerves, skipping lunch, or the champagne? Yes to all.

We start walking toward the church steps. My legs feel shaky, my skin clammy. *You made it this far. You're fine.*

"Paige, are you okay?"

*One foot in front of the other.* "A little shaky. It'll pass."

"Have you eaten anything today?"

"The wedding's at five o'clock. I figured I'd have dinner afterward at the reception."

"Breakfast? Lunch?"

*Keep going. You can do this.* "Yes to breakfast. I had two bites of toast. Then I had to get ready."

His hand goes to my bare back, a sizzling touch, as we mount the stairs to the church. A few other couples pass us on the way in. I think I know that woman in the purple dress.

"Why only two bites?" he asks.

"I told you. I had to get ready." *Just get inside. You'll feel better sitting down.*

He stops short, his voice low just for my ears. "If I'd known you'd barely eaten, I would've brought food in the limo. How're you feeling?"

I paste on a smile. "I'll be fine once we're inside."

"Pit stop."

He turns me around, and we walk back the way we came and then keep going down another block until we get to a falafel truck.

Spencer orders a gyro while I stare at the spinning meat, my stomach growling. I do like gyros. After he pays, he hands it to me. "My wife isn't showing up drunk off her ass at a church wedding."

"I'm not drunk. I'm just low on fuel." I take a bite of warm pita, meat of some kind, and delicious yogurt sauce. I chew and speak around it. "What if it weren't a church wedding? Then would it be okay for your wife to show up drunk off her ass? Say at a courthouse ceremony."

He kisses my forehead. "We're not going in until you've eaten at least half."

I offer him a bite.

He shakes his head. "I ate just before we left."

"You're missing out," I singsong, taking another bite of gyro.

He smiles. "At least you like to eat. And it seems you're not picky."

"I love food. All kinds."

He guides me a distance away as more people line up for the truck. "An ideal wife for a chef."

A secret thrill goes through me, even though I know he's just playing the fake-husband game. I take another bite, and sauce gets on the side of my mouth. I try to lick it. Spencer produces a napkin and wipes it gently for me.

"Thanks," I say, chewing happily. "You know who'd make an ideal husband for a successful innkeeper?"

"Who?" he says gamely.

"A strong silent type who understands I run everything."

"Hmm...wouldn't you rather someone who could match wits with you?"

I laugh. "No one can match wits with me, except maybe Wyatt, and he's out as a husband for obvious reasons. Did I ever tell you my parents were, I mean are, professors? One of them was and one of them is, as in right now."

"Yes, you mentioned it in your lap confessional," he says with a note of amusement.

For a moment I panic I might've revealed too much on the intimate champagne-fueled limo ride, but I don't have any dirty secrets, so I'm pretty sure I'm all good here.

I lift my chin. "It's true."

"I never doubt a lap confessional."

I give him side-eye. "Are you making fun of me?"

"I take lap confessionals with the utmost seriousness."

He's not smiling or laughing, so I go on. "Well, Mom is still a history professor. Dad's dead, but he was a brilliant math professor. He taught me calculus in middle school, and I knew classical history from Mom since elementary school. Go ahead, quiz me."

"Tell me the history of New York City."

"That's not classical history. But it was settled by the Dutch." I gesture around us. "This used to be all farmland. Hard to imagine with all the concrete and buildings, right?" I take another bite of gyro and realize I finished half already. I gesture to it. He did say eat half. It's entirely possible we're missing the wedding standing here chatting about history.

"You can finish it if you want."

"I think I will." I take another bite.

Spencer watches me eat for a few moments before saying, "You know, there's book smart and real-life smart. I suspect you're book smart."

"I'm both," I say around gyro.

He hands me a bottled water. I didn't even realize he bought that too.

"Thanks!" I lift a hand to open the bottle, but it's covered in sauce. "Could you open it?"

He opens it and hands it to me, using a clean napkin to wipe my hand off. "Can't have my wife walking in with sauce on her dress."

A rush of affection goes through me. I'd hug him if I weren't holding gyro wrapper and bottled water. "You're a great fake husband."

"You wouldn't really like the strong silent type."

"Says who?"

"You talk too much. It would drive you crazy not to get a response."

"Kayla married a strong silent type, and she can talk your ear off."

"Kayla's much sweeter than you. She probably finds the silence soothing and harmonious. You'd go nuts."

I narrow my eyes at him. "What makes you think you know me so well?"

He grins. "You mean besides when you told me your entire life story curled up in my lap?"

"I did not," I respond hotly. "We didn't even get to my college years."

His thumb brushes my cheek in a surprisingly tender gesture, his eyes warm on mine. It almost feels like Spencer actually likes me, not just pretending. His voice is silk. "I know you because I'm the same way."

Now I know he's messing with me. Spencer and I are NOTHING alike. We have zero in common. He's an arrogant player, and me, I'm the exact opposite—a caring, down-to-earth monogamous-type person.

"Why're you looking at me like that?" he asks with a hint of amusement. He's been entirely too amused at my expense today.

"Excuse me while I finish my gyro," I say pertly, not dignifying his ridiculous assessment of us with a comment. Even though it's obvious to anyone who ever met us there are stark differences. Wait until I tell Brooke about his comment. Boy, will she laugh her ass off.

He watches me chow down. Guess chefs really like to watch people eat.

"Paige, I hate to break it to you, but I don't think you and I'll be done after this wedding date."

I swallow audibly, nearly choking on my dinner.

He grins. "I like watching you eat too much. I have to cook for you."

I laugh and grab a napkin from the stash in his hand, wiping my face. "Show's over. How do I look?"

"Like a woman about to show up her ex with the best possible revenge—showing up with me."

I shake my head, a reluctant smile tugging at my lips. I feel a lot better now, and Spencer has been surprisingly agreeable, which helps. Still, I need to keep him in his place, or he'll walk all over me. "Spencer."

"Yes, Paige?"

I jab a finger at him. "Arrogance is not an attractive trait."

"Neither is drunkenness."

"I told you I wasn't drunk, only slightly buzzed due to an empty stomach. Besides, you bought me that champagne."

"Did I pour it down your throat?"

I smile. "No, you used a plastic flute, which I appreciated."

I toss the wrapper in the garbage, wipe my hands and face one last time with a napkin he hands me, toss that, and join him.

He crooks his arm for me, and we head back to the church. *Take two.* I'm well rested, well fed, and completely relaxed with my doting husband on my arm. At least he's doting for today. Tomorrow he'll morph back to the aggravating man he really is.

Or is this what Spencer's like when he takes an interest in someone?

It's too wonderful for me to question any of it. Tonight I'll just allow the adoration to continue. His for me, I mean. I know the score.

## 6

*Spencer*

I did the best I could setting us up as a newly married couple. The rest remains to be seen. Paige is sitting stiffly, a pleasant expression frozen on her face while the mushy vows happen up front. We found a seat at the back of the church and missed the boring sermon. I glance at her tightly clenched jaw, marveling at the strength it must take to watch someone you once thought you'd be with forever marry someone else. Despite her tough exterior, I've seen glimpses of a softer Paige. She did curl up in my lap and share stuff with me. I knew it was the champagne talking, but I wasn't about to push her away.

Anyway, she's vulnerable here. That's where I come in, protecting her vulnerable side. As long as we can get through the reception without fighting, everything will work out the way it should. I'll do my best, even if it means superhuman amounts of goodwill and patience. Ha. Honestly, I've enjoyed our time together so far.

The ceremony ends, and everyone erupts in cheers. Paige exhales sharply, taking my hand in a tight clasp and standing like the rest of the congregation.

The bride and groom walk down the aisle, holding hands and smiling. The bride is a perky-looking blonde with long hair, probably early twenties, and the groom, thirty-something, is a smug-looking asshole with dark short hair. Probably sporting a three-hundred-dollar haircut and Botox. His face is smooth and weirdly still.

"Congratulations!" Paige yells, boldly drawing attention to the fact that she showed her face.

Noah turns toward her, his voice excited. "Paige, you're here!"

The bride narrows her eyes and jerks him forward down the aisle. I agree with the bride. Noah sounded a little too happy to see Paige. Maybe the invitation wasn't to show Paige he could commit after she told him he'd die alone. Instead he could've had a genuine interest in seeing her. Not cool.

Paige turns to me. "He looked bad, didn't he? Kinda sallow with bags under his eyes."

Definitely no bags under his eyes. His skin looked tightly pulled across his face.

"Define sallow," I say, joining the crowd filtering out.

Paige hangs onto my arm and whispers loudly, "You know, like he was recently ill. He had a yellow tinge to his skin. Maybe he's jaundiced. And his hair is too short. He used to have thick waves, and now it's so short it looks straight with only a few spikes on top."

"He certainly can't compare to your husband."

"Ha!"

A few people look at us with that loud remark. She's wound pretty tight. We make it the rest of the way outside without incident.

Paige's eyes are glued to the happy couple accepting congratulations in a receiving line outside. I'm about to ask her if she wants to skip the line when she grabs my hand and pulls me into the line. Okay, so we're doing this.

Paige is muttering under her breath. I lean down and catch her saying, "Three weeks happily married."

She's rehearsing our story.

I give her hand a squeeze. "No one's going to quiz you in the reception line. Chill."

"I am chill!"

A few heads turn back to see who's so loud and unchill back here.

"Hi, Mitzi! Hi, Ford!" Paige says, smiling at the couple staring at her.

"Hello," Mitzi replies with zero warmth.

The couple look almost aristocratic with their perfect hair, designer clothes, and bland smiles. High society. They exchange a pointed look with each other before facing front. Probably surprised to see Paige here.

We're nearly at the bride and groom now. Paige's grip on my hand gets tighter. I'm not sure she's even aware of it.

"Are those the snobby friends who dumped you in the breakup?" I ask under my breath. "You're better off."

"Did I mention I like the strong silent type?"

"Is that your way of telling me to shut up?"

She smiles tightly and hisses, "Stop fighting with me. We're happily married three weeks."

I kiss her cheek. "My adoring wife."

Her cheeks pinken. "I can't wait for our culinary tour of Europe!" And then it's our turn. "Noah, so good to see you. Congratulations. This is my husband, Spencer Wolf. Spencer, this is Noah."

The bride speaks up. "Thank you both for coming."

"This is Bianca," Noah says absently, his eyes glued to Paige. "It's been too long. I didn't know you got married."

Paige holds up her hand with the gold band. "Three weeks. Still has that brand-new shine to it. We were just talking about our honeymoon. We're taking it after the busy summer season at my new inn. Congrats again!"

She sails forward, bringing me with her.

We take a few steps away, and then she throws her arms around my middle in a hug. I hug her back like a good fake husband, and then put my arm around her shoulders, guiding her away. I don't miss Noah's gaze following her. Too bad, asshole. You lost an amazing woman.

I glance down at her. "You want to walk to the reception or catch a ride? I can call our driver back."

She beams up at me. "I'd love to walk, but my heels aren't exactly made for—ah!"

I grin at her in my arms. That's right. I swept her right off her feet. "Is this better?"

She buries her head in my chest. "I can't believe you picked me up."

I start walking. It's three blocks to the hotel. Not a lot of people are on the sidewalk, so it's easy going.

She giggles. "Everyone saw, right?"

"I assume your scream drew attention, but then they realized it was just your husband sweeping you off your feet."

"This looks so romantic."

"I told you I was the best choice for your wedding date. Seriously, could Audrey do this?"

She laughs and rubs my chest. "You're so warm."

"That's because I'm getting a workout carrying a woman down the street in the heat of July."

She smacks my chest. "Okay, put me down. I can take a hint. I'll just take off my heels and walk in my bare feet."

"Are you crazy? The sidewalks are hot enough to fry an egg."

She sighs. "I guess I'm stuck like this."

"You're actually lighter than you look."

"Spencer! That is an insult wrapped in a compliment."

"What? You have big hair and wide cheeks. It just seemed like you had more heft to you."

"Heft! That's it. Put me down." She wriggles, and I tighten my grip on her. "Put me down!"

"Shh. Now you're drawing the wrong kind of attention. Did you forget we've been happily married for three weeks?"

"Well, the honeymoon's over!"

"The honeymoon hasn't even begun."

She goes still in my arms. "You mean our pretend culinary honeymoon in the future, right?"

I look down at her. "What did you think I meant?" Then I realize why she went still. She froze up thinking I was going to pressure her into that one-night thing. She's the one who put the idea in my head, and now it's stuck there.

"Paige, we're not hooking up tonight. Not even if you paid me."

She sputters and then glares at me. My gut tightens, the blood rushing through my veins. It's really hard not to feel lusty with a beautiful woman in my arms, even if she is pissed off half the time.

No. She's vulnerable. This is a difficult time for her. Only an asshole would take advantage of that. Don't be that asshole.

I continue on, imagining the trip of my dreams as a distraction from my lusty thoughts. "Anyway, back to our honeymoon, my beautiful wife." She relaxes in my arms, absently rubbing my chest. Just the smallest of compliments softens her up. Good to know.

"Yes?" she asks in a near purr. My sexy little kitten. With claws. I like that.

"Our culinary tour would start in Paris, naturally, and then on to San Sebastián, Spain, hit up Barcelona, and circle back up to France again to Lyon, then on to Italy, first in Bologna and then Florence."

She sighs. "That sounds amazing. I love traveling. I went glamping in Tanzania, snorkeled the Great Barrier Reef in Australia, and toured Japan, but I've never been to Europe. Seems silly since it's closer. My ex planned those trips. Never mind. Where've you visited?"

"I haven't traveled as much as I'd like, just along the East Coast. But that's the two-week culinary tour I've always wanted to take."

"I'd agree to a honeymoon like that."

"You would?"

"Mostly for the tapas." She's focused on the important thing—the food.

I smile, my arms full of sexy woman, my mind fully engaged, and my heart beating a little faster. Because I can picture us taking the trip of my dreams together.

～

*Paige*

I'm enjoying being Spencer's fake wife so much I haven't paid much attention to Noah and what's-her-name. Okay, I had a twinge when they were announced officially for the first time as Mr. and Mrs. Miller in the grand ballroom of this five-star hotel. Mostly because I thought that would be me—Mrs. Miller. Still Miss Winters. No, today I'm Mrs. Wolf. That sounds much better than boring old Miller.

During the reception's cocktail hour, I made the rounds chatting up my former friends. I told them all about the inn, as well as Spencer's amazing cooking, and invited them to visit with the VIP treatment. I've been handing out business cards like confetti, but I still haven't managed to snag some alone time with the best man, Alex. He's at the head table with Noah and the bride. I need to wait until he's alone to pitch the inn for an article in his travel magazine.

Now Spencer and I are sitting at a table of people we don't know. We just finished a delicious dinner of prime rib. Noah seemed surprised to see me, so I assume it was his bride who parked us with some great-aunts and uncles on Noah's side. I guess that's better than putting me with the friends who cut me out of their lives the moment Noah and I broke up. I hate to admit it, but Spencer's right. They were never my real friends.

Spencer leans close, his arm around the back of my chair. "Now that you've enjoyed your second meal in two hours, would you like to dance?"

I turn to him. "Closer to three hours, and I was hungry."

"I could see that."

"We don't have to dance. Plenty of married couples are hanging at their tables. Look around."

His words run hot against my ear, and I suppress a shiver. "I'd like to dance with my wife."

I shift, meeting his eyes up close, and smile, a fizzy, bubbly feeling of happiness rising in me. Like champagne, only better. Who would've guessed the arrogant man I'm constantly butting heads with could turn out so wonderful? I'm sure this behavior will all go away after tonight, but there's no reason I shouldn't enjoy it. A brief stab of melancholy clouds the bubbly feeling for a moment as I wish for the impossible—more of this wonderful man. I'm being silly. This isn't real.

He takes my hand, guiding me out of my seat and on the short walk to the dance floor. It's a slow song. The bride and groom are out here along with other couples.

Spencer's hands go to my waist. I put my hands on his shoulders, keeping some distance between us. It's important to keep some boundaries in our little game of pretend.

His hand goes to the small of my back, drawing me closer and closer until we're pressed indecently close. A flash of heat goes through me.

"Spencer," I whisper.

He leans down by my ear. "Hmmm?"

"Maybe a little distance would be more appropriate."

"Why? Are you getting ready to grind on me?"

"No!"

He does a subtle grind. "I can tell you want to."

I smack his shoulder, smiling despite myself. "You're being bad. No one else is grinding."

He guides me in a slow circle, so I can see Noah and the poor woman who became his wife. "How about now? Any bride-groom grinding?"

"Please."

Noah catches my eye and mouths *hi*.

*Eww. Focus on your new bride!*

I meet Spencer's sky-blue eyes, which seem darker in the hotel ballroom. More like sapphires. "You have nice eyes."

"Thanks, so do you. Whisky eyes."

"Oh, thanks."

"And your hair reminds me of caramel. The swirl of it, the lighter brown with darker. Pretty."

That's color straight from a salon. I'm normally just plain dark brown like my sisters, but I keep my mouth shut. "Thanks. Do you see most things in terms of food or drink?"

"Not at all. I would describe your mouth as big."

"I would describe your mouth as snarky. I like the beard.

Thanks for growing that for me. You're much hotter now." I shut my mouth with a snap. Didn't mean to admit that out loud.

"Is that so?"

"From a revenge standpoint."

"So I was only medium hot before."

"You weren't…uh, can we talk about something else?"

"How're your feet?"

"My feet?"

"Aren't those heels the reason I had to break my back carrying you three blocks?"

I narrow my eyes. "You know, for a guy who puts in the work to be a doting husband, you sure do say a lot that rubs me the wrong way."

"I have that effect on people. I've been told I can be abrasive. It's just my subtle sense of humor."

"Does anyone ever laugh?"

"I laugh on the inside."

"Maybe try to keep those jokes to yourself, eh? Might have better luck making friends."

"I've got plenty of friends."

"Well then, better luck with women."

"Never had a problem with those either. I got you, didn't I?"

He dips me suddenly, and I squeak in surprise. Then he pulls me back up, close, his eyes smoldering into mine. My breath comes harder, the comeback on the tip of my tongue deserting me.

His hand cups my jaw, his lips meeting mine. A jolt rushes through me on contact just like last time. It's over too soon as he pulls back to look at me. "Beautiful."

I have no words, dazed by all I'm feeling.

He continues our dance, guiding me in a slow sway. I feel someone staring and catch Noah's eye. Revenge is sweet. Noah sees me madly in love with my new husband.

I'm beginning to believe this is how Spencer treats someone he really cares about, and I love it. I'm tempted to ask him how much of this is real when the song ends, and a fast song starts, blasting a thumping beat.

"You want to keep going?" Spencer asks over the music.

"That's okay. Maybe I'll get a glass of champagne and kick back at the table."

"Perfect."

We walk off the dance floor.

"Could you get me a whisky?" he asks. "I'm going to stop at the restroom."

"You got it. A whisky to go with your wife's whisky eyes."

He puts both hands to his chest and staggers back. "How did I get so lucky?"

I laugh at his antics and wiggle my fingers at him. He closes the distance, grabs my wiggling fingers, and kisses them. My breath stutters out.

"Go easy on the champagne," he says.

I roll my eyes and yank my fingers from his grip. "Just one glass. Besides, I'm well fed now. I won't be climbing into your lap again."

He gives me a slow sexy smile. "That part I didn't mind. I just prefer my partner sober. How else can you appreciate my charm?"

"Is this a riddle?"

We grin at each other. I head for the bar, and he heads for the exit, in search of a restroom.

I join the line at the open bar, enjoying the music. Hard to believe how much I dreaded today, ever since I got the invitation in the mail. Yet only four weeks later I'm perfectly fine. Better than fine, I'm actually enjoying myself.

"Paige, I'm so glad you could make it."

I turn to find Noah and the best man, Alex, standing behind me. I glance around for the bride. Her back is to us across the room as she hugs some people at a table in the corner.

I smile. "Of course. We've both moved on. It's good to see everyone again." I turn to Alex, a tall blond with high cheekbones. He could've been a model; instead he inherited a media empire. "How've you been, Alex?"

He smiles his dimpled smile. "Can't complain. You look good, Paige. And I just heard you got married. Congratulations."

I lift my hand with my fake wedding band. "Sure did. And now I'm running a B&B in the country about an hour outside the city. It's a beautiful old Dutch farmhouse from the eighteenth century that my sister and I converted into the Inn on Lovers' Lane. Super romantic. That's actually the name of the street. Lovers' Lane. We specialize in private inner-circle weddings and elopements, but really it's great for any couples looking for a getaway. Maybe you and Christina would like to visit."

"We broke up."

*Oops!* "Sorry."

"I'm not."

"You could come out and see for yourself. VIP treatment. I'll reserve our best suite for you. And the food is amazing. Fresh from our garden and the local farmers' market. My husband is the consultant chef for everything. He's the best. Not that I'm biased. You can read for yourself in our reviews. I think it would be perfect for readers of *Leisure Travel* too."

I whip a business card out of my purse, and he takes it, tucking it into his pocket.

"Sounds like a nice break from the city," he says. "Only problem is I'd be out of place at a romantic place like that. My only love these days is for my dog, Trixie."

"Enough shop talk," Noah says sharply, glancing around. Probably checking on his bride. She's still across the room, chatting with her guests and hugging them.

I smile at Alex, ignoring Noah's rudeness. He always wants to be the center of attention. "We're dog friendly. Bring her along. My sister's golden retriever, Scout, visits all the time." I pull out my phone and show him a picture of Scout lounging on the back patio of the inn.

Alex warms, smiling as he pulls out his phone. "Trixie's a golden retriever too." He scrolls to her picture.

"Gorgeous! It's a doggie date."

"Great!"

Noah sighs, like this is the most boring conversation in the world. Whatever.

After we get our drinks, Alex and I step out of line to keep talking about the inn and the dog-friendly town I live in. Seems the dog-friendly angle was a winner with Alex. I hope he'll agree to come out. I just know he'll love it. Noah tags along, silently listening in and sipping his drink.

"Email me more info and some pictures," Alex says to me. "I'll pass it along to my travel editor. I'd better catch up with my date."

I beam, nearly bouncing with the sudden lightness in me. "Thank you so much. I'll do that. Great to see you!"

Alex nods and walks away. I turn to Noah. "I should find Spencer." I can't wait to share the good news. We can toast with our drinks. I glance around but don't see him.

"Can I talk to you for a minute?" Noah gestures me around the corner from the bar to a quiet alcove.

"Uh, okay." I follow, telling myself there's nothing he can say that will hurt me anymore. Maybe he wants to finally apologize. Maybe he's devastated that I've moved on so successfully and realizes he made a terrible mistake letting me go. I'll be discreet and won't rub it in his face. I'll just be quietly vindicated on the outside while doing a small jig on the inside.

"Paige, I know why you're here."

Heat rises in my cheeks. I hope I didn't come off as a cold shark closing in on prize bits for my business. I'd like to think I also wish him well in life. Well, maybe not that far.

He lowers his voice, his eyes intent on mine. "You still have feelings for me. I told myself if you came today, it meant we still had a chance."

My jaw drops. "Noah, you just got married."

"She's pregnant."

"Oh-kay." I feel suddenly awkward standing in a quiet alcove with my ex, knowing way more than I should about Noah's private business. I stare at the whiskey in my hand, thinking of Spencer. "I should go."

He speaks in a fierce whisper. "I wouldn't have proposed

otherwise. I've never felt about any woman the way I feel about you. That's why I had to invite you. And you came."

I grimace, thoroughly disgusted by him. "Go back to your wife."

"I know you feel something. You were making eyes at me on the dance floor."

"I promise you I wasn't."

He leans close, his voice soft. "I love you."

My jaw gapes.

He continues in a coaxing voice. "We're both married now, but that doesn't mean we can't see each other sometimes. I'd really like to meet up again. Did you get a room at the hotel?"

I'm tempted to throw these drinks in his face, but I rise above that pettiness. I whisper to him, mindful of the fact that we're at his wedding reception. His poor wife. "Grow up, Noah. You're a husband and soon to be a dad. It's your wedding day, for God's sake! Try to do the right thing for once."

I stride away, fuming. I can't believe I almost married this sleazeball! How could I have been so blind?

Just then Spencer comes into view, heading straight for me, a small smile on his handsome face. My heart kicks harder. What am I doing getting excited over Spencer? He's only pretending to be my doting husband. Didn't my lack of judgment with Noah teach me anything?

We meet up again at our table. Spencer takes his whisky and pulls out my chair for me with the other hand. "Sorry it took me a while. I got waylaid in the hallway by one of the great-aunts from our table. She wanted me to help her flag down a taxi."

"No problem." Apparently, Spencer has a soft spot for women in need. That's probably why he's here with me today, but that's not me at all. I was only briefly vulnerable over a man who never deserved me. I set my champagne down on the table and take my seat, still fuming over Noah. Such a rat.

Spencer wraps his arm around the back of my chair and

starts playing with a lock of my hair. I'm tempted to lean into him, but I resist.

"I'm not a woman in need," I inform him.

"Nobody said you were."

"I can flag my own taxi."

"Never doubted it."

I let out a breath and try to focus on my good news—things couldn't have gone better for the inn, and I permanently put Noah behind me. Everyone here saw me as a successful business owner and a happily married woman. Isn't that the best revenge? To be better off without Noah and friends? I couldn't have pulled it off without Spencer. The contrast between him and Noah is so striking I can't lump them together in the arrogant player category anymore. Spencer's honorable, gallant even. A knight in shining armor comes to mind.

I turn to Spencer. "I successfully pitched the inn to the media guy. He told me to email him all the details." *And I permanently put Noah behind me.*

"That's great!"

"Yeah."

He leans close to my ear, his voice low. "Why do you look pissed off?"

I'm quiet for a moment. First, because I thought I had a pleasant expression on my face. Second, do I really want to share that I almost married a total sleazeball? My eyes get hot. I feel so foolish. Noah's a cheater; he's always going to be a cheater.

Spencer straightens, his shoulders pulling back. "It was your ex, wasn't it? What happened? Did he insult you?"

He looks like he's about to avenge my honor, and I love him for it. Whoa. I didn't even have any champagne yet. I didn't mean love. I meant like him so much, and I'm so grateful to have him on my side.

A lump of emotion lodges in my throat. "You're awesome."

He glances at my drink, sees it's full. "Is that your second glass?"

"No, I haven't had any yet."

"Why am I awesome?"

I sigh. "I don't know. It's a surprise to me too."

He gets in my face. "Stop avoiding my question. What happened?"

I shift to whisper in his ear and tell him every sleazy word from Noah's mouth.

He pulls back to look at me, his jaw tight. Then he stands abruptly. "Excuse me, I'm going to kick some ass."

## 7

I jump up, grabbing his arm and whispering fiercely, "I'm embarrassed enough that I almost married the guy. Don't make a scene."

"He came on to my wife!"

"Shh!"

"Nobody comes on to my wife, especially when I'm around to do something about it."

*My knight in shining armor.* I give his arm a tug in a futile attempt to make him sit down again. People are staring. "Can we please sit and talk about this calmly?"

"Unacceptable."

I hang onto his arm tight. "I love that you want to avenge my honor, but this isn't how I want it to happen. What I'd really like is to spend time together just the two of us. How about we ditch this place and have a night out in the city?"

He stares at me for a long moment. "Is that what you want?"

"Yes, please."

He cocks his head. "Because fun with me is the ultimate revenge."

I smile. "Now you're getting it. Let's go, okay?"

He exhales sharply. "Fine, but I'm kicking his ass in my mind."

I pat his well-formed bicep. "I so appreciate it. How are you at karaoke?"

He cracks a smile. "Let's find out."

*Spencer*

I saw a different side of Paige tonight. She's relaxed, fun, and still tough as nails. I'm beginning to appreciate a strong woman. She could've let her ex ruin the night. And for a minute there, she was definitely in full-on regret mode. Now she's back, better than ever.

We're at this cool basement lounge with multicolored lights aimed at a small stage for the karaoke singers. There's also a bar and a smattering of wooden tables for people to sit and watch the brave belt out tunes. Paige and I covered a whole slew of duets from "Don't Go Breaking My Heart" to "Shallow." I give us a ten out of ten for volume and a two for musicality. It's fun to let loose with her. I love seeing her smile light up her beautiful face.

Now we're sitting at a table, drinking water alongside whiskey. It was her idea to keep hydrated while sipping whiskey and belting out tunes. She says it's better for our vocal cords and we'll avoid a hangover. I have the feeling she's had some experience with this.

"Last song before close!" the bartender announces.

A bachelorette party rushes the small stage to claim the song.

"Should I call the driver, or do you want to keep the band going at another bar?" I ask.

Her eyes roam over my face before she smiles brightly. "Let's keep it going. Tell the driver he's off duty for the night."

"He's our ride home."

She waves that away with a *pfft* sound.

"Eventually we have to get home. I've got work tomorrow."

She leans close. "Plenty of time. Did I mention I have a

condo in the city where we can crash for the night?"

I stare at her, my heart kicking up. *Is she still thinking about that honeymoon night?* "No."

She nods once, looking pleased with herself. "I bought it with Noah, and since he's got more money than he knows what to do with and felt guilty for leaving me a week before the wedding, he signed the title over to me. My consolation prize. We co-owned it, and now it's all mine."

That's surprisingly generous for her cheating asshole ex. I'm sure selling would've been the smarter move, unless he's rolling in dough. Is that what Paige is used to? There's no way I can match that. It hits me that Paige hanging onto their old place means she's still stuck on Noah, and that pisses me off. He doesn't deserve her. He's a coward with no honor.

I go on the defensive. "Why do you hang onto the condo? Still wallowing in your memories with him?"

"No!"

"Then why?"

She shakes her head. "You ask too many questions." She looks toward the bar. "You want another drink?"

"You should sell your condo. Buy another place in the city if you want, but as long as you have it, you're hanging on to your memories with your ex."

"Well, look at you, Mr. Relationship Expert. Tell me, what was your longest relationship?"

"Irrelevant."

"A week?"

I clench my jaw. "A month."

"Ha! I knew it."

"It's not like it was my fault. Things just didn't work out for one reason or another. You don't see me hanging on to old relationship stuff."

"I'm not hanging on to old stuff. It's an investment."

"And how often do you use your investment?"

"That doesn't matter. The value will only go up."

So damn stubborn this woman.

I try for a reasonable tone. "I know you stress over the inn having enough business. Why not sell the condo and give yourself a cushion? Then you don't have to stress about the inn's business so much."

She looks to the stage, where "Summer Nights" from *Grease* is currently being murdered by the bachelorette party.

"Well?" I prompt.

She pulls me close and whispers in my ear, "Because if the inn fails..." She shifts away and speaks normally. "I can pick up my old job with a place to land." She used to sell real estate here.

Clearly, Paige has commitment issues—she's not all in on her new life in Summerdale—which makes me relax a bit. She won't be upset if I'm not great at relationships or whatever this is between us. I don't know why things don't work out with my relationships. I'm very lovable.

I can't let the condo thing go. "If you go all in on the inn, you're more likely to succeed. I'm going all in on my restaurant once I get the funds."

"Going for gold when you're broke is different than going for a new life when you already have something you've built."

"I'm not *broke*. You're hanging on to the past."

She gives me a deadpan look. "I take it from this lengthy discussion that you don't want to go back to my place with me. Fine. Call your driver and go home. I'm staying in the city."

Was that what I was doing? Arguing my way out of spending more time with her? I've been having a great night and don't want it to end. Ah, hell. I got jealous that she hung onto something she had with her ex and screwed up the good part.

"I don't want to go to a condo full of your ex memories," I admit.

She gets in my face, smiling. "Du-u-ude, I put his stuff out on the sidewalk for him. That place is all me. You're so cute when you're jealous."

*Cute? Puppies are cute.*

"I'm not jealous," I say in my most dignified manly voice.

She cups my jaw, her eyes dancing with amusement. "Uh-huh."

I put my hand over hers, turn it, and kiss her palm. "You threw his shit out the door, didn't you?"

She smiles mischievously. "I'll never tell. Anyway, my place is on the Upper West Side. We could hang there for the night. Two-bedroom, two-bath brownstone with a rentable basement apartment."

"Are you trying to sell me your condo or invite me over?"

She grins. "Make me an offer."

*Am I really going to do this?*

*Are we still in vulnerable Paige territory? The wedding must've been an ordeal for her.*

"How're you feeling right now?" I ask.

She bounces in her seat. "Great."

"Yeah?"

"Yeah." She grabs my arm and tugs, trying to get me to stand up.

"Okay, you twisted my arm." I stand, rubbing my arm like her tugging was an awful twist. "But I don't have anything with me." *Do we need to stop for condoms?*

"I've got an extra toothbrush. Don't worry."

She heads toward the exit of the karaoke bar. I toss some cash on the table and follow her, the blood rushing through my veins. If I push aside all that honor crap and worrying about taking advantage of a vulnerable woman, I can admit it —I want her fiercely.

I catch up with her outside, where she's hailing a cab.

"I'm not hanging onto my ex," she says.

"Okay."

"Really. I have a tenant in the basement apartment, which helps with costs. I know it would make better economic sense to sell, but I'll never find such a great place for the price I paid again. I snatched it up the moment it came on the market. Buy low, sell high. That's the way to win in the real estate market."

A cab pulls up, and she gets in. I follow. She gives him the address and slumps down in the seat, looking relaxed.

"Isn't it always a sell-high market here?" It seems

Manhattan real estate prices never go down.

"I think it'll go up more," she replies. "It makes it easier to hang on knowing that." She turns her head toward me and smiles. "You're more fun than I thought you'd be."

"You're more relaxed than I thought possible."

"When I don't have to run the show, it's easier to relax. Champagne and whiskey helps."

"Hours apart, thank God, or I'd be peeling you off the sidewalk."

She curls into my side. "Or I'd be in your lap, oversharing."

"I never did hear about your college years."

"Did you go to college?"

"No, I apprenticed to an incredible chef right out of high school. I didn't want to waste time or money on culinary school. The best teacher is experience."

"I suppose if you have the right person to work under, that's true. But if you were just a fry cook at a diner, that's a whole other story."

"True."

She smiles up at me. "Climb into my lap and tell me your life story."

I chuckle. "You're definitely feeling the whisky if you think that's a good idea."

"I had just enough to be relaxed. Two whiskeys, plenty of water, and that yummy popcorn."

I half sit in her lap to show her how heavy I am.

She shoves me. "Oh my God, you're heftier than you look. Get off me!"

"But you invited me." I return to my seat with a sigh. "Talk about mixed messages."

She pokes my chest. "That doesn't mean you get out of sharing for an off-lap confessional. I told *you* stuff."

"Completely unprovoked. I didn't ask you a single question."

She scowls. "Rude. I don't think you're going to be a fun houseguest."

I glance toward the driver, who's quietly humming along

to a song in a language I don't recognize. I keep my voice low. "Fine. I'm an only child. My parents are a traditional couple. He works; she keeps house. Dad wants me to join him in the car sales business. He owns a few dealerships around the area. I went my own way. He's unhappy. Mom doesn't understand. I'm happy. That's my life in a nutshell. The disappointing son who triumphed on his own."

She smiles, her eyes soft. "Triumphed, huh?"

"Yes, triumphed. I work at something I love. I'm the head chef in a restaurant with an owner who doesn't mind me taking the lead." I shoot her a significant look for all the trouble she's given me in that regard. "And I'm saving for my own restaurant one day. Doesn't matter that I haven't achieved the dream yet. What matters is that I have a dream."

She pats my bicep. "Well said."

The taxi pulls to a stop. I offer to pay, but Paige insists she's got it. "I'm not traditional," she tells me.

"Good." Wouldn't want to be dating my mom. Not that Paige and I are dating. I'm not sure what we're doing at the moment, but I can't resist her.

She meets me on the sidewalk and pulls a keychain from her purse. "Here we are, home sweet home. God, I've missed this place."

I follow her up the steps to the entry door. "You more of a city girl?"

"Not especially. I grew up in the suburbs of New Jersey."

"Which is known for the wilds of nature."

She laughs and opens the door. "Hey, there's plenty of beautiful spaces in New Jersey. Where I grew up in Princeton had lots of trees, flora, and fauna."

"Fauna, huh?"

"You know, native stuff. Birds, squirrels, deer, bears, the occasional bobcat." She opens another door, steps inside, and gestures ahead. "Living room." It's a comfortable-looking space with an overstuffed gray sofa. She takes my tux jacket from over my arm and sets it on the sofa. She walks across the space to a small galley kitchen separated by a half wall. "Kitchen. Want something?"

*You.*

I shove my hands in my pockets. "No, thanks."

"Me either."

She walks over to me, hips swaying, a gleam in her whiskey eyes.

My heart pounds, desire coiling within me. She's temptation personified.

She steps into my personal space, her eyes sparkling. "I had a wonderful time tonight all because of you."

My voice comes out gruff. "Me too."

"You were the best fake husband I could've asked for. In fact—" She wraps her arms around my neck. "I don't want this night to end."

Does she want me or the doting fake husband? I have to be sure. Because we're not the same person.

I keep my arms at my sides, though I'm so tempted to wrap them around her sexy body. "I told you we didn't have to follow through with a honeymoon night. I'm not your husband. That was an act of revenge, and I played the part. You get that, right?"

"Yes."

"Gloves are off," I say by way of warning. "That guy is not me."

She grins and grabs my hand, leading me toward the stairs. "You can just be you now."

I follow her upstairs, anticipation racing through me. "You don't like me."

"I like parts of you."

"Is that supposed to be a compliment?"

She stops short at the top of the stairs and holds a finger to her lips. "Shh. Don't ruin it by fighting with me."

"Who, me? I'm very easy to get along with."

She gestures me on. "Follow me." She walks confidently down the short hall to her bedroom.

I rush her from behind, wrapping my arms around her. Not even a squeak. She leans back and smiles up at me. "That's more like it."

This is going to be fun.

~

*Paige*

"Unzip me," I say, giving Spencer my back. I kick off my heels. We're in my room, and I know what I want—him.

"No kissing? No foreplay?"

I shoot him a look over my shoulder. "Don't tell me you're a romantic."

"Why bother taking the dress off at all?"

He bends me over and hitches my dress past my hips, gathering it in his fist at the small of my back. Excitement races through me, my nerves tingling, my breath coming harder.

He lets out a low groan as he traces the edge of my black lace panties with one finger. "So sexy," he murmurs.

"What're you waiting for?"

He pulls me back up and turns me to face him, his hand cupping the back of my neck. "That mouth," he says before his mouth crashes down over mine. A dizzying wave of lust has me clutching the front of his shirt. He pins me back against the wall, hitching my leg up and grinding against me.

I break the kiss. "Oh my God. Just take me." All that fighting we did before was because of this—need that was denied. No more.

He kisses down the column of my throat, his teeth closing around the cord of my neck. My breath stutters out. His mouth returns to mine roughly, his nimble fingers unzipping my dress. He slides it off, and it pools to the floor.

I slip off my backless bra, a clever push-up with clear halter straps.

"Paige," he says in a guttural voice.

"Your turn. Strip."

He slowly shakes his head, pulling me close and kissing my collarbone, the round of my shoulder, and finally my breast, lingering there. I thread my fingers through his hair as he sucks hard, desire pulsing between my legs.

He switches to the other side, suckling, his hand on the small of my back, keeping me close. Need claws at me. He gives me one last lick and drops to his knees, sliding my panties down and off. He places a tender kiss on my sex before rising to his feet and kissing me again.

"So beautiful," he says reverently.

My lips part in surprise. I didn't think he'd be so sweet.

His arm bands around my waist as he kisses me, guiding me to the bed. My knees hit the mattress, and he pushes me back on it. I reach for him, but he drops to his knees, spreads my legs, and places one leg over his shoulder and then the other, exposing me to his view. I stop breathing. He lowers his head and gives me one long lick. I gasp, my hips jerking. *Did not expect this much from him.*

"I thought it would be hard and fast," I manage as he tastes me again.

He looks up at me. "Still talking? I'll have to do better."

And then he renders me speechless as he dives in for more. My hips arch to his rhythm, his fingers thrusting inside me, adding to the intensity. I'm panting, my release hovering near. White-hot pleasure steals my breath as I writhe under him. I'm on fire. Hot coiled pleasure consumes me, ratcheting up, up, up. Higher and higher.

He clamps a hand on my hip, holding me still as he works me, and I explode in a rush of sensation, fire shooting through my limbs. He stays with me, guiding me through every last wave of pleasure until I collapse. *Whoa.*

I hear him shift, getting to his feet. I can feel him staring. My eyes are closed, and I'm too spent to make the effort to open them.

"Mmm," I manage to say. That was a lot of tension I just said goodbye to. I wish I could always feel like this. "Better than any massage."

He cups me between the legs, and I cry out, still sensitive, my eyes flying open. Just a slight amount of pressure from the heel of his hand sets off another rush of pleasure. I moan softly.

"Condom?" he asks.

"Nightstand drawer."

He starts unbuttoning his shirt, his eyes smoldering into

mine. I maneuver to a sitting position to help him, mostly by shoving my hands into the opening of his shirt and feeling him up. I can't resist tasting the muscular lines of pecs and chest and abs. He groans and tosses the shirt to the side.

I go for his buckle, but he pushes my hands away and makes quick work of stripping. His erection springs free, and I wrap my hand around it.

"Paige, I can't wait." He pushes me back.

That's when I remember the condom, scrambling over the bed to fetch it from my nightstand drawer. I toss it at him and lie back, spreading my legs in invitation.

He groans long and low. Suddenly he's on me, taking me in one slow thrust. A rush of sensation makes my breath catch. He fills me, and it feels so right.

He rests on his forearms and strokes my hair back from my face. "You good, beautiful?"

My heart squeezes. He's checking in with me. "I never suspected you had such romantic depths."

He bites my earlobe and gives it a tug. "No one's ever accused me of being a romantic before."

I run my hands all over him, loving the feel of all that heated skin.

"I'm going to fuck you hard now," he says.

I throb at the words. "Yes. Do it."

He drives into me again and again, hard and fast, his breath harsh by my ear. I lift my hips to take him deeper, and the next thrust hits just the right spot. My nails dig into his shoulders, pleasure rocketing through me with every thrust. *Yes, yes, yes.*

My grip on his shoulders loosens, and I cry out, the orgasm ripping through me.

Our eyes lock, my breath still coming hard. His blue eyes reflect stark need and something more, recognition. We're similar animals. I see that now too. A match beyond the physical. It scares me because we fight too much.

"Fuck me," I say.

He groans and hikes my leg up, opening me more as he pounds into me. I gasp, shocked at the intensity. Too intense.

"More," he demands. "Give me everything."

Sensation overwhelms me. Speech is impossible. All I can do is take it. Everything he gives. I tremble, fever hot, my breath coming in sharp gasps. His fingers give me a gentle stroke, strumming lightly, and I go off, rocking helplessly. He thrusts deep again and lets go, gripping my hips tightly to him. We share every pulse of sensation as close as two people can be.

Slowly he eases back from me, lowering my leg. I curl on my side, overwhelmed by all he made me feel. It was supposed to be just a release. This was too much feeling of every kind.

He rolls me to my back. "Don't go cold on me."

I shove his shoulder. "I'm not cold. I'm wiped out. It's been a long night."

One corner of his mouth lifts. "Good." He leaves the bed and heads out, probably for the bathroom down the hall.

I sigh and fling my arms wide. What do you do when you have the best sex of your life with a man you're completely incompatible with in real life? One night of a doting Spencer doesn't change all that went before. He warned me that wasn't him. He was playing a part tonight. Though he was generous and kinda romantic in bed. He checked in to be sure I was okay.

I don't even know if he wants a relationship. A month isn't a great track record. Let's see if he sprints out the door.

He returns, and I watch him warily. Is he going to get dressed and make an excuse to go?

He grins and climbs onto the bed, covering me with his body and propping up on his forearms. "Is this the part where we talk about the relationship?"

I look away, my throat suddenly tight, hot tears stinging my eyes. He's joking, and I'm feeling way too much. "No."

He cups my jaw and turns me back to him. "I was kidding, but just so you know, I'm not a cheater. If I'm done, I'll let you know and then move on. Cheaters are weak."

My eyes well. I think I'm in love.

## 8

*Spencer*

I can't sleep. I thought everything was good, but I can't get Paige's teary face out of my mind. It's past dawn now, and she's still sleeping. The guilt is killing me. I took advantage of a vulnerable woman. She was upset over her ex. The whole point of me being her date was as a defense against that, and then I took it too far. Even if we did have a good time, I should've drawn a line. I was caught up in the moment, driven by lust. I'm made of stronger stuff than that.

Dammit. It kills me that her eyes got so teary after sex. Obviously she regretted it. And before that, she looked so vulnerable, curled up on her side away from me, her voice choked when she spoke. Through the whole wedding and reception she showed such strength, but underneath it all she was vulnerable. She said it was a long night. We stayed out until three a.m. after she'd been worked up for days over her ex. I should've taken better care with her.

I look over at her sprawled on her stomach in a deep sleep.

I quietly get out of bed, gather my clothes, and step out in the hall. After I dress, I go to the kitchen and find a notepad on the counter with a pen. A note is more personal than a text. I can't be faulted for that. My gut clenches, and I ignore it. I'm doing the right thing. Besides, I have to get back to Summerdale for work.

And I can't bear to see her tears.

I start the note with: *Paige, it was a mistake.*

I crumple that up. I don't want to make her cry more. Mistake sounds bad. Next!

I think for a moment. *Paige, I had to go to work.* Crumple that up. Lame, even if it is true.

*Paige, I had a great time. It's not you. It's me. I never should've—*

Crumple. No, no, no.

Finally, I come up with the perfect way to step into neutral territory that will allow everything to smooth over between us. Satisfied, I head back upstairs, fold the note in half, and leave it propped on her nightstand.

*Paige*

I wake feeling well rested and energetic. I crack open my eyes and peer at the clock on the nightstand. Oh, wow, it's noon. I was really wiped out. Well, it was an emotionally exhausting night with the wedding, reception, and then going out with Spencer, my former enemy. Ha-ha. I spy a note propped on my nightstand, and I'm immediately suspicious. Do not even tell me he bailed after last night.

I roll over to check. Not there. I know he slept over. He got into bed and pulled the covers over us. I was so relieved he wasn't ditching me after sex. My feelings for him are so new and intense, I would've been devastated if he had. That's the last thing I remember before I conked out. I sigh. Back to reality.

I sit up, grab the note, and push the hair out of my eyes, prepared for the worst. My jaw clenches tight as I read.

Paige,

The timing wasn't right. Sorry about last night.

I hope we can be friends.

Spencer

*Dammit, Spencer!* I crumple the note in my hand. A classic *it's not you, it's me* excuse. *Timing.* What timing wasn't right? We had a great time together followed by great sex. Everything was awesome on *my* end. Only, apparently, it wasn't for him. I throw the note as hard as I can. It lands on the mattress an annoyingly short distance away.

*Sorry? He's* sorry *about last night?*

*Friends?*

I grab my pillow and scream into it.

Then I march to the bathroom for a hot shower. Spencer Wolf will regret the day he ditched me after a hookup.

~

By late Sunday afternoon, I'm back at the inn. Brooke's already checked out our weekend guests, so there's nothing left to do but clean up.

All I can think about as I'm scrubbing with all my pent-up anger is that Spencer doesn't get to ditch me. I made an impulsive move on him after an emotionally exhausting day. It's over now because it never should've happened in the first place. I made a mistake never to be repeated again. My choice from start to finish.

"You okay?" Brooke asks as we put away the cleaning supplies. "I don't think I've ever seen you scrub so hard."

"Just tired. I stayed out late for karaoke last night."

Normally, I'd confide in my sister, but I gave her a hard time for getting involved with someone on our payroll before. Dammit. I should've listened to my own very smart advice and never gotten involved with our caterer/consultant chef. Unprofessional. Embarrassingly so. *Can I still fire him after having sex with him?*

She tilts her head. "You seem more tense than tired."

"Probably a touch of a hangover."

"Ah. That's the good kind of tired to have after fun with your friends."

*One friend. No, an acquaintance I hope never to see again. Only how do I explain why I let the best chef in town go?*

We walk into the kitchen to take off our gloves and wash our hands.

Brooke gives me a bright smile. She's always deliriously happy these days. *Must be nice.* "I'm going to head home. Tomorrow we can go over the marketing plan Sydney made for us. We still need to build a solid customer base."

"Absolutely. Oh, I almost forgot the best news—I spread the word about the inn with my friends in the city last night, and I'm pitching it to an editor at *Leisure Travel*. I'll email the editor right after this."

She gives my arm a squeeze. "Awesome! You're always on top of everything. Sounds good. Bye!"

She sails out the door, and I follow slowly behind her to lock up, suddenly depleted of energy. I move to the nearest cushy beige sofa in the living room and flop down, too exhausted to make the trip to my apartment upstairs. My mind flashes through my time with Spencer again, trying to find the moment where it went south. I can't figure it out. There was no bad moment. The only thing I can conclude is he just wasn't that into me. Maybe I wasn't the doting fake wife he needed.

I force myself off the sofa. Enough with this wallowing. I'm a woman of action. I head upstairs and prepare a pitch to send to Alex for *Leisure Travel*. Once I finish that to my satisfaction, I hit send, and then, since I'm already in marketing mode, I email my former friends from the wedding with photos of the inn, a link to our website, and a warm invitation to stop by. There. All loose ends from last night are tied up.

I close the laptop and drop my head in my hands, thoughts of Spencer crowding my mind again. That stupid note.

How dare he apologize! The nerve, the *audacity*.

I'm going to confront him right now and demand he take back his apology. He can't be *sorry* about last night. He can agree with me that we're better off going back to status quo—boss and contract employee. I'm a mature adult. Sometimes you have a good time with someone, and then it's over, and that's fine. You move on.

I need his address. Wait, he said he had to work today at The Horseman Inn. They're closed on Mondays, so I'll just wait to confront him tomorrow on his day off with no witnesses. I grab my purse, fully intending to text him to meet up, but when I pick up my phone, there's a text from my youngest sister, Kayla. It's a picture of her English bulldog, Tank, curled up with a light brown tabby kitten. Under that, it says *Look! We got Tank a kitten and he's in love!*

I'm ridiculously relieved for the distraction. I text back. *Adorable! How did this happen?*

Kayla: *I went to the animal shelter to look into fostering a puppy for the Best Friends Care program and fell in love with Simba. That's the name she came with, but I think it suits her.*

Me: *No puppy?*

Kayla: *The puppy was too rambunctious for Tank's tastes. Tank's a laid-back dude.*

*More like lazy.* I like the Best Friends Care program to train shelter dogs as companions for veterans with PTSD. I didn't know they had puppies in need of fostering. This is a sign.

Me: *Are there any more puppies?*

Kayla: *I'm not sure. You should head over there because there was a lot of interest.*

Me: *I'm there.*

She sends a string of celebration emojis.

This is exactly what I need to get my mind off men who do stupid things. I've been wanting a dog, a warm, furry bundle of unconditional love. And it's for a good cause.

A short while later, I'm at the animal shelter in town. It's a red-sided building behind the veterinarian's office. I was here once before for the groundbreaking of the shelter when Brooke and I were trying to get the word out about the inn with locals. We left brochures in Dr. Russo's office next to the architectural model of the building, which is now built thanks to numerous fundraisers and generous donors. I'm pretty sure my brother, Wyatt, provided the largest donation, but he prefers to remain anonymous.

I open the glass door and step inside a cheery space. The floors are glossy hardwood, probably to make accidents easy to clean up. There's a small reception desk and a young woman with long blond hair sitting there. I'm guessing she's in high school.

She smiles. "Hi, I'm Deena, can I help you?"

"Yes, hi. I'm interested in fostering a puppy for Best Friends Care."

Her heavily mascaraed eyes widen. "Ooh, you came just in time. There's only one left." She pops up from her seat and walks around the desk. "Everybody went nuts for the golden retriever puppies. We took in the mother when she was pregnant. Don't know who the father is, but the pups sure look pure golden retriever. Come on." She gestures for me to follow as she heads to the back of the shelter.

I follow her past an examining room, another office, and into a large kennel. There's a row of metal crates, as well as two large corner spaces closed off with baby gates.

She gestures to one of the gated areas with metal folding chairs. "This is where we have cuddle time with the dogs. Go in and have a seat, and I'll bring Green Collar out to you."

"Green collar?"

"They're so young we just color coded them. Figured their owners would name them."

I nod and head toward the cuddle area, climbing over the gate and sitting on a metal chair. My breath catches as I spy the bundle of soft golden fur in Deena's arms. He's wearing a thin green collar and looks around curiously.

I meet her at the gate, and she deposits the puppy in my arms. He immediately rests his front paws on my shoulders and licks my neck. I pet his soft little head, and he licks my cheek, his back end wriggling with his wagging tail. "Oh my goodness, aren't you precious!"

"This is a boy dog. You'll need to bring him back for neutering. Dr. Russo does those free for foster parents."

I hug his wriggling body close, loving the little fur baby in my arms already. "So what do I need to do to foster him?"

"Exactly what you're doing. You just love on him, introduce him to different people and things so he'll be well socialized. Once he's six months old, you'll need to bring him to one of our trainers. After he passes his therapy dog certificate, then one of our Best Friends Care volunteers will get to work on finding his forever companion."

"When does that usually happen?"

"For a puppy, they usually go to their forever home when they're a year old. It depends on the special needs of the veteran."

"And he's how old now?"

"Nine weeks. So you'll most likely get to keep him for ten months."

I look down at Green Collar, and his big brown eyes gaze into mine. "That's a long time. What should I call you?"

He licks my cheek and wriggles. I set him down, and he stands on my leg, begging to be picked up again. I scoop him up and cuddle him close. "I'm calling you Bear because you're just a little lovey bear!"

"You need to fill out some paperwork, and I'm required to say that it will be hard to let him go, but please know you are helping a veteran regain a solid footing in life. It's an act of pure love to foster a puppy."

My eyes well. "I've got a lot of love to give." I didn't realize how much until this moment. The dog smiles at me. I swear! I rub his little body.

Deena gestures toward the door. "Right this way, ma'am."

I stiffen. *Ma'am?* Do I really seem that old to her? My big three-oh birthday flashes through my mind, the wedding invitation, crying for days.

Spencer ripping that invitation in half. My delight.

*Nope. Not thinking about him.*

I follow her, cuddling Bear close. Who needs a man when you have a cuddle bug like Bear?

## 9

*Spencer*

It's been a week. Hopefully, Paige and I can have a civil conversation. I'm catering another wedding at the inn on last-minute notice. This one is a true elopement, where the couple spontaneously decided to get married after check-in yesterday. I had to shift my work schedule to make it happen, and I only did that because I want to have a face-to-face conversation with Paige. Part of me thought I'd hear from her earlier, at least acknowledging my note. It would've been polite.

But then I started thinking she was too upset to reply, which was worse than thinking she was rude to ignore the gesture. How much damage did I do taking advantage of a vulnerable woman? I still don't know. She's been busy decorating the wedding pergola in the backyard with the help of her sister, and I haven't gotten to talk to her yet. Paige looks more relaxed today, dressed casually in a black and white striped cotton dress with thin straps that ends below the knees. Usually she wears crisp blouses and tailored pants or skirts. Like a professional. What made her loosen up? Was it our amazing sex? Maybe I'm not the villain here after all.

I'm making tartlets from peaches I picked up this morning at the farmers' market when she finally stops by the kitchen. She appeared from the opposite direction than I expected. She must've taken the back staircase to her apartment from outside before coming through the inn.

She stands a distance away in the nearby dining area, holding a bundle of golden fur in her arms. "How's it going in here?" She doesn't sound upset at all. A great sign.

I wipe my hands on a dish towel and approach her. "It's going well. I've got an arugula salad with heirloom tomatoes, a few appetizers, and peach tartlets. Jenna sent over a small white wedding cake as requested." Jenna owns Summerdale Sweets, the local bakery.

Paige pets the dog in her arms, smiling at it. "Good."

Strange. Usually Paige would want to know exactly what appetizers I had planned. It's not like her to be hands off. Maybe since it was a last-minute wedding, she's going with the flow.

"Whose dog is this?" I ask, giving the puppy a scratch behind the ear.

"Mine. I'm fostering him while he's in training to be a therapy dog." She speaks to the dog in a singsong voice. "This is Bear because he's a little cuddle bear."

I stare at her, surprised at how loving she sounds. And looks too. It's almost like she's holding a baby close. A vision of Paige as a loving mother flashes through my mind, and warmth spreads through me. I don't know why that appeals to me so much. It's not like I'm ready for marriage and kids. I'm twenty-nine. That's for far in the future, once I'm a successful owner of my own restaurant.

I focus on Bear, letting him sniff my hand. He licks it. "You sound happy."

She smiles and meets my eyes up close. My heart kicks harder. "I am."

She forgave me. I knew a note was better than a text. Still, I need to be sure. "So we're good."

"Mmm-hmm," she says, smiling down at Bear.

I suddenly want that smile on me. I want to see her again, outside of work. "How about you and Bear come over to my place tonight for dinner? We did talk about me cooking for you before. I can make some primo meat for him."

Her expression turns blank, and she blinks a few times.

*Did I surprise her with the invite?*

She recovers herself. "Uh, things are crazy right now with the inn and everything."

"Oh, sure. Well, let me know when you get a break."

She flashes a quick smile that doesn't reach her eyes. "Bye." And then she walks out the back door with Bear.

I watch as she greets the groom, who pets Bear, and then moves back toward the inn, her eye catching mine through the window. There's no fire in her eyes directed toward me, nothing but a serene look of a woman who has everything she needs to make her happy. And that doesn't include me.

Dammit. I want back in. I don't care if she's fighting with me or having dinner with me. I want to matter to her again.

The moment she walks inside, I speak up. "Peaches weren't right for tartlets. I'm going to substitute apples."

"Sounds good," she says, not even slowing her stride as she heads upstairs, probably to check in with the bride.

My gut does a slow churn. Menu changes used to make her flip out. Now she couldn't care less what I do.

"What's wrong with the peaches?" my assistant Rick asks.

I shake my head. "Nothing. We're still using them." I just wanted to see if Paige was paying attention. It's like she couldn't care less about our night together.

I'm the one who can't get it out of my head.

The next time I see Paige, she's on the deck just outside the kitchen with Bear on a leash. Bear's sniffing around while Paige is doing something on her phone.

I step outside. "Hey, how's it going?"

She doesn't bother to look up. "Getting the music set up. The bride wants some retro sixties music. Think she's going for a hippy vibe, which is perfect since Summerdale was founded by hippies. It's on our website. Maybe that's what attracted her to the inn. She goes by Rainbow."

"Cool." I shove my hands in my pockets and clear my throat. "It's good to see you."

She taps her phone a few more times.

"After the wedding, maybe we could get a quick drink."

She scoops up Bear. "Busy, but thanks."

"Paige, wait."

She stops and looks at me blankly. Where's all that fire that used to be directed at me? Or the adoring look for her adoring fake husband?

Heat creeps up my neck at my pathetically needy thoughts. "Are you mad at me?"

"Why would I be mad at you?"

"I don't know."

She lifts one shoulder and readjusts the bundle of wriggling puppy in her arms. "I don't know either. See ya."

"See ya," I mutter.

She goes back in the house, and I stay behind a moment. I hang my head. What does a guy have to do to get noticed by the woman he had amazing sex with? *I* know it was amazing. *She* knows it was amazing. So none of that matters now?

We need to talk.

I'm so distracted watching Paige set up for the wedding I can barely focus. Thankfully, my assistants work efficiently around me. I pass off most of the cooking to them.

By the time the wedding is set to begin, I step out onto the deck to watch. Usually Paige will back off for the ceremony and watch from over here. Brooke's in place by the pergola to take pictures. Paige turns and walks toward the deck. Bear must be in her apartment because it's just her. This is my chance to finally talk.

But she walks right on by, heading into the inn. Okay, maybe she's getting the bride. I'll catch her on her way back.

My assistant Sara pokes her head out the back door. "Are you still doing the tartlets?"

"You and Rick do it this time. I trust you."

"Sure?"

"Yeah, I need to talk to the owner about something."

"Okay, but we don't have the magic touch with crust that you do."

"Use iced water when you're forming the dough. Don't let it dry out before you're ready to use it. Put a damp cloth over it if you need some time."

She repeats my orders to herself under her breath, nodding. "Okay. Will do."

She's not professionally trained. Neither is her husband. She learns from experience just like I did. Paige agreed with me about experience being a good teacher while she was sharing in her lap confession before the wedding last week. She told me she earned a degree in economics, but didn't really learn banking until she did it. Same with real estate and now running an inn. We're both hands-on, hard workers.

The back door opens, and Paige appears with the bride, who's wearing a white cotton dress with crocheted daisies that falls to her ankles. She paired it with white high-top sneakers.

"You have a beautiful day for your wedding," Paige says to her.

The bride is silent, walking toward the pergola.

Paige glances over at her, saying something under her breath I can't hear. They get to the small red runner that leads to the pergola, and Paige taps her phone. The wedding march begins.

The bride slowly walks down the aisle.

Paige turns and heads back toward the deck. God, she's beautiful. The sun hits her hair, bringing out auburn highlights that fall in a sensual wave to her shoulders. I don't know why we fought so much before. All I want to do now is wrap my arms around her.

She climbs the steps of the deck. "Our third wedding. Looks like our theme is working."

"I wonder how many will be elopements."

She joins me, looking out toward the wedding. The bride is next to the groom now. "Depends on how many impulsive people show up."

"You might be responsible for upping the divorce rate. Maybe you should offer an impulse divorce package."

"Not funny." She keeps her gaze on the wedding. "It's romantic."

I scoff. "Romantic is another word for pretend. The guy just does all this fake stuff to please the woman like when I played husband for you."

She shakes her head. "This is why you're single."

I open my mouth and shut it again, stung by the remark. Since when do I care about being single? I enjoy the freedom.

She glances up at me. "I ripped your note in half and threw it away. Wasn't as satisfying as ripping my ex's wedding invitation, but it was up there."

*She* is *mad at me. Well, at least I matter to her.*

*What is wrong with me?*

I turn to her. "Would it have been better if I said it to your face?"

"You left, so I wouldn't know."

"I had to get back to Summerdale for work."

"Right."

Just then the bride picks up the bottom of her dress and tears down the aisle toward us, her eyes wide.

"Oh, shit," Paige mutters under her breath. "Rainbow! What's wrong?"

The groom chases after her, dressed in a button-down shirt with a bow tie and jeans. "Rainbow! Wait for me!"

Rainbow dashes past us and into the inn. The groom follows behind her.

Brooke catches up to us on the deck. "She said she couldn't take the pressure."

"Cold feet," Paige says.

"Should we go in there and calm her down?" Brooke asks.

Just then the groom steps outside, running a hand through his short cropped brown hair. He's young, early twenties. "She said she just needs to check in with her tarot cards. I can wait. No rush, right?"

"Of course," Paige says.

"Can I get you a drink?" Brooke asks.

"No, thanks. I'm going for a smoke." He heads back toward the koi pond, which is a secluded spot surrounded by tall plants.

The sisters have a quick silent communication. I have a feeling the bride's not coming back, but I don't want to be the one to say it.

The roar of a van reaches us as it accelerates down the street. Paige leans over the deck railing to see. "Oh my God!"

She turns back to us. "Rainbow just took off in her VW van!"

Brooke worries her lower lip. "Do you think she's coming back?"

Paige slowly shakes her head.

"One of us should tell the groom," Brooke says.

"What if he's so mad he doesn't want to pay for the wedding or the room?" Paige asks. "They didn't have a credit card, so I said we'd take cash."

Brooke hisses out a breath.

"I'll tell him about his bride," I say. "Man to man. He won't want to lose face by looking like a wuss slinking out. Then I'll make him pay up."

"Oh, Spencer!" Brooke exclaims. "That would be wonderful. Thank you so much."

"I should do it," Paige says. "I'm the innkeeper."

"Let me do this for you," I say. "After the dust settles, we can have that drink."

"Drink?" Brooke asks, looking between us. "You two?"

"I told you I'm too busy." Paige heads down the steps, probably to go talk to the groom.

I follow close on her heels and grab her arm, halting her. "He'll take it better from a guy."

She looks at my hand on her arm. "Let go."

"I get the feeling you're mad at me."

"Wow, you're a genius."

I warm at the response. So much better than her blank expression. "Okay, I already apologized for that night. Why exactly are you mad?"

"Why exactly are you apologizing?"

I step close enough to whisper in her ear, "Because you were vulnerable, and I took advantage. You looked like you were about to cry."

"I was not about to cry. I never cry over stupid things."

I lean back to look at her, offended. "So now I'm a stupid thing?"

"The whole night was stupid. Bringing you to my ex's wedding, even going to the wedding. Stupidest thing I've ever done."

"Stupider than sleeping with me?"

She turns away, crossing her arms. "I don't want to talk about it."

"Why? It was amazing. You have to admit that much."

She's quiet.

"The timing was bad with your vulnerable state, but that doesn't mean—"

She whirls. "What? That we can still hook up? No, thank you."

"I asked you for a drink or dinner. I didn't say get in my bed."

Her chin lifts. "Might as well have. You invited me to dinner at your place. An intimate setting. You think I haven't been here before with a guy?"

"Not with me."

She huffs. "What do you want?"

*You.* "I don't know."

She exhales sharply. "I don't have time for this. I'm going to talk to the groom."

I grab her arm, pulling her back to me.

She jerks her arm away. "Stop grabbing me!"

"Stop running away."

Her eyes spark fire, and lust rushes through me, a matching fire in my veins. She's battling with me because there's something here. Passion. The fact that it's still there after we've already been together is awesome. I never feel more passion afterward.

"You still want me," I say.

"I don't need anything from you."

"You do. You need me in your life."

"Bye, Spencer." She strides off to the koi pond to find the groom.

I follow at a slow pace. I'm *not* chasing her like a desperate guy. We're just not done talking yet.

She appears a moment later from behind the tall plantings surrounding the pond. "He's not here."

I look around the yard. We were so busy fighting we didn't notice the groom slipped away.

"Brooke! Did you see Greg go by?" Paige yells.

Brooke looks up from her phone. "No. I thought he was in the meditation area."

Paige hurries back to the inn with Brooke and me on her heels.

"He couldn't have bailed without paying," Paige says. "We're out a lot for the wedding, and they booked two nights."

"I'll check their room," Brooke says, rushing ahead and up the stairs.

Paige peers into the empty den and then crosses back to open the front door, checking outside for him. I peer over her shoulder.

Suddenly a black Fiat convertible races down the street. Is that—

"My car! He stole my car!" Paige runs outside. "Hey! That's my car!"

The car speeds by in a blur. "Shit."

Paige's hands form fists, and she lets out a primal scream. "Ahhh!"

I turn to her. "Guess that drink's sounding pretty good about now."

"Go home!"

She turns on her heel and marches back inside.

I follow because she needs me.

## 10

*Paige*

I am in *hell*. Not only did the bride and groom split on us, I just found out the groom totaled my car. He survived the crash, fortunately. I'm at the police station in town, filing a report with the chief of police, Eli Robinson. Eli is my sister-in-law Sydney's younger brother, so we're family. He's all business now, which I appreciate. My mind is tallying up the costs from the wedding, the lost revenue from the room, and replacing my car. The car is five years old, so I'll only get the current value of the car back after my deductible. That means I have to cough up extra money for a new car.

Dammit, I loved that car. It was my gift to myself after my first big real estate sale. I sold a two-story penthouse to a wealthy older couple, who then spread the word about how much they liked working with me.

"You want to see the car?" Eli asks. "They towed it to Murray's. Mr. Murray drove the tow truck and said it was a lost cause."

I shake my head. "No, thanks. Where did Greg crash it?"

"Not far from Murray's, actually. He was speeding all around the area, looking for his girlfriend, and did another tour through town after dark, speeding down a winding road and hitting a telephone pole. It came down on the car. He was lucky to walk away. Broken arm, couple of broken ribs, and a concussion."

I suck in air. That sounds awful. It's really dark here at night. There's only a couple of streetlights. Most places it's pitch black. Here I was thinking I was in hell, but it's much worse for the poor dumped groom. It's hard to stay mad at Greg when I think about his day—ditched at the altar and then nearly killed in an accident. Of course, it *was* a stolen car, but his bride took their van, and he wasn't thinking straight. My keys were conveniently out on the dining room table after I made a quick trip for puppy clean-up solution. The day had been such a flurry of activity I forgot about them until the car was stolen.

I finish up the paperwork and pass it over to Eli. Then I stand and shake his hand. "Thanks so much for your help."

"Just doing my job." He claps my arm in a half hug. "Good to see you again, Paige. How're things going at the inn besides this?"

I sigh. "We're getting there. Not quite in the black yet, but showing signs of life."

"Things can only go up."

I smile and turn to find Spencer leaning against the doorway, his arms crossed. He was so quiet I almost forgot he was here. Brooke could've driven me here, but Spencer insisted.

He gestures for me to go ahead of him out of the office. He follows me out, holding the front door open for me as I walk out of the old Victorian house that now serves as a police station. I'm not sure why he's sticking with me now after bailing on me before. I guess he took that friends thing seriously.

He unlocks his black pickup truck, and I climb inside. As soon as he gets into the driver's seat, I say, "Thanks for the ride."

"No problem." He backs out of the lot and heads toward the inn. "You've had a hell of a day. And after last weekend—"

"Don't remind me." Bad enough I had to live through seeing my ex marry the woman he cheated on me with, but then I made a huge mistake falling for my doting fake husband. The truth is, Spencer's just another guy only interested in the hookup, not the relationship. Whatever. I'm not dwelling on that. I've got enough to deal with.

"Don't worry about the catering cost for the wedding," he says. "I'll comp it and donate the food to a shelter."

"A donation sounds good, but I'm still paying you. Today wasn't your fault. It's my inn running elopements, so it's my responsibility."

"Running brides too."

I sigh.

"Too soon?"

I take in a deep breath, not up to engaging with him. "You exhaust me."

"That's better than taking advantage."

I sit up straighter. "When did you take advantage?"

He stops at a red light and faces me. "That night we were together. You were vulnerable after dealing with your ex."

"I admit it was a rough night, but then things turned around."

He gives me a skeptical look.

"So you think that night was all your doing? I'm the one who invited you back to my place."

"It was both of us, but I should've been the one to draw the line. *I* wasn't vulnerable."

"Spencer, I had a great time with you that night. I actually felt happy for once, and then you—"

"What?"

"You ruined it."

He gestures toward me. "This is what I'm saying. So I apologized, and now I think we should start fresh. Maybe not tonight, but when you're up to it, we can have dinner."

"And then what?"

"What do you mean and then what?"

"And then we hook up again?"

"If you want."

I reach for my last shred of patience. The man makes no

sense. Lovers, friends, lovers maybe? "And what do *you* want?"

He doesn't answer. The light changes, and he hits the accelerator.

I look out the window, too wiped out to deal with him. We're quiet the rest of the way home.

He pulls into the driveway of the inn and finishes the conversation as though no time has passed. "I guess I want you."

"You *guess*?" I open the door of the truck and get out, slamming it behind me. "I *guess* I'll pass."

"We'll talk when you're not so upset."

I want to kick his stupid truck, but I'm wearing sandals. Instead I lift my chin and turn on my heel, walking away with my dignity intact. I'm so over bringing clueless guys up to speed. No wonder Brooke scared men away for so long with her fake-fiancé story. Men are frigging exhausting.

I let myself into the inn and flop down on the living room sofa. My phone chimes with a text from Brooke, and she races downstairs a moment later.

"She left a one-star review!" she exclaims.

Dammit. This is bad because we only had two other reviews, a five and a four star from local guests. This brings our average way down. I click over to the review Brooke just texted me. The runaway bride took the time to leave a one-star review for the inn on a major travel site. I read it, my jaw dropping.

*Horrible atmosphere, uncaring staff, and all they do is push their elopement package in your face. My boyfriend felt pressured to propose. Now he dumped me after cold feet. Save yourself some heartache and avoid this B&B if you're in a relationship.*

"Can you believe this?" Brooke exclaims. "She's going to scare away all the couples we're trying to cater to!"

"We never pressured anyone! And *she's* the one who got cold feet."

Brooke paces the living room. I'm too exhausted to pace.

She stops. "Okay, she's probably just upset and left a

drunk review, right? Maybe we can get in touch and ask her to change it."

"We have more right to be mad than she does. She ditched us with the bill."

She gives me a wry look. "We're in the hospitality business. We have to think bigger picture."

I click over to our website. Is it too romance focused? I don't think so. There's pictures of the inn and the rooms on the front page. You'd have to click over to the elopement and weddings tab. I set my mouth in a firm line. "We're not begging for a good review."

"I'll just politely ask, okay?"

My shoulders slump. I can't deal with another problem today. "Okay. You call her. You're nicer than me."

"Done."

I hug her and tell her goodnight. She heads home to her cozy cottage with her new husband, Max.

I drag my ass upstairs to my apartment and open the door. Oh shit. My throw pillows are torn to shreds, cotton puffs everywhere. Bear trots over to me, tail wagging, a piece of cotton stuffing stuck to his muzzle. Gee, I wonder who's responsible for this? At least my place wasn't ransacked by a robber or a vengeful bride.

All I can do is laugh. It's either that or scream.

Audrey invited me to ladies' night at The Horseman Inn, and I'm trying very hard to relax. Wine should help. Everyone's been very welcoming.

"Could I get another one, please?" I ask the bartender, Betsy. She's young and cool in a retro way with her pink hair and multiple piercings paired with an outfit that looks like it's from the '50s. A white cardigan cut to her midriff and a poufy turquoise skirt with a hand-embroidered poodle. Makes my usual business casual outfits seem stiff.

"You got it," she says, uncorking a delicious French sauvignon-blanc. I have my older brother, Wyatt, to thank for the impressive wine and beer selection. It's been his pet project ever since he married Sydney, the owner of this place.

Audrey leans forward by my side. "I'll get another pinot grigio, please."

Jenna chimes in from my other side, "Look at you two, actually drinking wine at our Thursday night wine club." She has a dry martini.

I smile. Audrey explained this used to be "book club" night, but no one ever read the book, and they just kept drinking wine, so Sydney renamed it Thursday Night Wine Club, and then everyone switched to other drinks. Can't put a label on this group.

"Audrey and I are rebels," I say, which makes Jenna and Sydney giggle. Audrey does look like a prim librarian, so I guess it could be funny to think of her as a rebel. I've found her refreshingly honest and sharply intelligent. We love to talk books.

My younger sister Kayla is here too and jumps in to defend me. "Paige went her own way becoming an entrepreneur, which is an act of rebellion in itself."

Wait, I'm the one who seems too prim to be a rebel? Is that why they're laughing?

"I'm a rebel for sticking to water on wine night," Sydney says with a self-satisfied smile. She rubs her belly. "I'm sure the baby will appreciate it." She's four months pregnant and talks about it every chance she gets. My little niece or nephew will be here next January. I'm happy for her, but it's not so interesting to hear about pregnancy nonstop. I'll be more into the kid once he or she arrives.

"Audrey's a rebel for writing the Great American Novel," I say. "That takes guts to pour your soul into a book and put it out there for the world to read." Not spilling any secrets, her friends were asking her about her book earlier.

Audrey rocks her head side to side. "Well, I wouldn't call it rebellious so much as brave."

We all clink glasses in a toast to Audrey. The ladies are big on toasts every time they get a fresh drink or when someone says something profound.

Wyatt walks in, his eyes glued to his wife. He's carrying a small gift bag.

"Hi, Wyatt!" Kayla says. "What're you doing here on ladies' night?"

He glances at her. "Hi, everyone." He gives Sydney a kiss and hands her the gift bag. He's hard-core devoted to his wife.

She flushes, her eyes bright. "What's this?" She opens the gift bag and pulls out a tiny white onesie that reads Little Devil with devil horns.

Kayla and I exchange a look of amusement. When Wyatt and Sydney first met, she called him Satan. As in he was evil. She couldn't stand him at first. Once they started dating, it became a term of endearment, and he started calling her she-devil. Now they're having a little devil.

"Are you the least concerned you're putting an evil hex on your unborn child?" Jenna asks.

"I love it!" Sydney exclaims, throwing her arms around Wyatt's neck. Her eyes are shiny with tears.

I look away, unexpectedly choked up.

Kayla wipes under her eyes. "I'm so happy for you guys!"

Wyatt lifts a hand from Sydney, welcoming Kayla to join them in the hug, and she rushes over for a group hug.

Audrey takes a long swallow of wine, and I do the same. Jenna's smiling and texting. Probably telling her husband, Eli, to put a baby in her too.

"How's work?" Audrey asks me.

"Awful."

"Why? What happened?"

I tell her the whole story of the runaway bride, the groom who stole my car and totaled it, and our one-star review.

"This happened last Saturday, and I'm just hearing about it now?" Audrey asks.

"I didn't want to bother you with my problems. I would've told you at book club, but it was cancelled." The air conditioner broke at the library, so it temporarily closed while a new air conditioner was installed.

"Sweetie, you don't have to wait until ladies' night to tell me stuff. Call me anytime."

"Really?"

She squeezes my arm. "Of course."

A weight lifts from me. I have my sisters close by, but it's nice to know I have a friend too. "Thanks. I know I shouldn't let it bug me so much. Eventually, we'll get more reviews, and it'll all even out." I sigh. "Honestly, I'm rethinking the whole wedding angle."

Kayla pipes up, returning to her seat, "But it's so romantic! Brooke's wedding there was wonderful. Just because you had one dud doesn't mean you should scrap the whole thing." She holds up a finger. "Let me get in touch with my wedding planner. Hailey has a contact at *Bride Special*. Maybe they'll be willing to cover the next wedding you have booked, and the whole thing will turn around."

I sit a little straighter. *Bride Special* is a national bridal magazine. That could be just what we need. I haven't heard back from the editor of *Leisure Travel* yet, and Alex's schedule has been too busy to take me up on my offer to visit the inn. Never hurts to have more publicity.

"That would be awesome. Thanks, Kayla." I turn to Audrey. "Now we just need an engaged couple. Know anyone?"

"My friends are all married, except you."

"Right." I take a drink of wine.

"Any chance you'll get engaged in the next couple of months?" she asks.

I nearly spit my wine. "No."

"You could do an elopement dream wedding giveaway promo!" Kayla exclaims. "The brides will be lining up to win."

Kayla is easily excitable.

"But isn't the point of an elopement to keep it small and low key?" I ask. "What would make it a dream elopement?"

She's quiet for a moment. "Chocolate from a really good chocolatier?"

"I can get you good chocolate," Jenna says.

Kayla gestures to her, like what she said.

I smile at Jenna, owner of Summerdale Sweets. "You know you're my go-to person for sweets."

"Ooh, a designer gown!" Kayla exclaims. "Even an eloping bride would love a special gown."

"Sounds expensive for us," I say.

Kayla deflates.

"I'll think about it," I say.

Sydney turns to me. "Speaking of weddings, I heard you had a wedding date with Spencer. Rehearsal for the big day?"

I flush. Did Spencer share about our wedding date? Or Audrey? It's hard to keep your private life private in a small town like this. I'm still used to the anonymity of the city.

Wyatt's arm is around Sydney, so it's like I'm talking to both of them. He lifts his brows.

"How did you hear about it?" I ask.

Kayla lifts a hand weakly in the air. "I might've mentioned it. Spencer was asking me about you and your ex, so that's how I found out he planned to be your wedding date."

My jaw gapes. "Spencer asked you about my ex? What did you say?" Kayla is honest to a fault and the worst oversharer.

Her light brown eyes widen, making her look innocent. I know better. "Nothing bad! It was all Noah's fault between you two, and that's exactly what I told Spencer."

I want to ask her if she spilled how devastated I was, how I couldn't get out of bed for a week and dragged my ass for months, but I don't want to share my pathetic story with the group.

"So-o-o, how's Spencer as a wedding date?" Sydney asks brightly.

All eyes are on me. A rare blush takes over as I remember just how wonderful he was that night, but then after—

"Fine," I say.

"Only fine?" a deep voice says from behind me. I jump and turn to see the man I can't stop thinking about.

Spencer gives me a wry smile. "You seemed pretty satisfied that night."

I suck in air.

The women titter.

"Watch yourself," Wyatt warns.

I roll my eyes at my overprotective brother. He's two years older and acts like he's responsible for me.

A riot of emotions runs through me seeing Spencer again. He was there for me for my ex's wedding and stuck by me through the whole runaway-bride ordeal last weekend. There's something very appealing about a man who stands by your side when things go to shit.

*Don't be so easy on him! He also dumped your ass after hooking up with you.*

I look him up and down in his chef's uniform of white shirt and pants. "Shouldn't you be cooking something?"

A slow sexy smile graces those sensual lips, and my heart kicks harder. "I'd like to cook dinner for you. How's tomorrow night?"

I suddenly notice the normally chatty ladies are absolutely silent, everyone paying close attention to the two of us. I'm in slippery territory agreeing to an intimate dinner with him, and I don't want a repeat hookup and bail.

"Things are really busy at the inn," I say. "I've got a lot on my plate. Stuff I can't put off."

"Oh-h-h," a woman's voice says from behind me, like she's disappointed in my answer. Probably Kayla. She loves Spencer. They used to work together when Kayla was a waitress here.

"I'll fix it," Spencer says simply. "Whatever you need. Then we can have dinner."

"Now who does that sound like?" Sydney asks Wyatt. My brother is the ultimate buttinski, fixing everyone's problems whether they want him to or not.

"It's an admirable trait," Wyatt says. "I approve."

"Just one more reason to run very far away," I tell my brother.

"Don't be an idiot," Wyatt returns.

"You'll want to rephrase that," Spencer says to Wyatt with

a hint of threat in his voice. "Though I appreciate the support."

Wyatt inclines his head, one alpha boss to another. "Paige, when a guy offers to fix your problems, it's an act of love."

Sydney hugs him sideways and kisses his cheek. He smiles widely and gives her a squeeze.

Spencer coughs. "Don't know if I'd put it that way exactly."

Shocker. Spencer is freaked over the L word. I want a guy who's not afraid to have an actual relationship. I hate that I still have all these feelings for him. Could he possibly want more than just another hookup? If I knew for sure, if there was a reason to hope—

I just don't want to be twice burned.

"Don't worry about it," I tell Spencer. "I've got everything under control. Just need to do the work to get things back on track."

He searches my expression, glances around at the rest of the group, and takes a step back. "My break's over." He strides toward the employee door that leads to the kitchen.

I finish my wine in one gulp.

Audrey rubs my back and speaks in a soft soothing tone just for my ears. "He comes on strong, but I think he means well."

I want to tell her the sordid details of why I want nothing more to do with Spencer, but there's too many witnesses, including my brother, who'll raise hell on my behalf. He'll kick ass for me or any of my sisters and now Sydney too. He'll be a great dad. I hope he and Sydney have a lot of kids so he'll be focused on them instead of us fully grown adults. It's a little embarrassing to be thirty years old with an overprotective big brother.

"It's complicated," I tell Audrey.

She perks up. "I'm all ears."

"Later."

She nods and smiles. "Gotcha."

Conversation veers over to Audrey's novel again. Her friends are insanely curious about it, probably because she refuses to share any details until it's done. She says it'll stifle her creativity. I'll get it out of her, one bookworm to another.

A short while later, everyone heads home.

Audrey walks with me to my rental car. "You want to tell me what went down with Spencer?"

"You want to tell me what your book's about?"

She gets close and whispers, "It's about a soldier battling demons from her past."

"Like supernatural demons?"

"No, it's realistic. PTSD. And it goes back through generations of military service in her family. A military family saga."

"Wow. Interesting. So—"

"That's all you get, which is more than I've told anyone else. What's up with Spencer? What happened on your wedding date?"

"He was the perfect fake husband all night. We had a good time."

"And?"

"And then we hooked up, and he left before I woke, like a pussy."

"Awful."

"Here's what's really awful—he left a note apologizing. An apology after sex! Obviously, he thought it was a mistake. And the only reason he's asking me to dinner at his place is for a repeat. Think I've learned my lesson there."

She tilts her head, looking thoughtful. "I don't know. He seemed sincere tonight. Maybe he regrets moving so fast, and he's trying to dial it back to a low-key date so you can get to know each other better."

I snort. "This isn't a rom-com. He's not going to suddenly appear—"

"Paige, wait up!"

Audrey giggles while I stare in shock as Spencer jogs through the parking lot to me. His hair is disheveled like he ran his fingers through it and pulled.

"Hi," he says, a little out of breath when he reaches me.

"I'll see you later," Audrey says, wiggling her fingers and heading for her shiny red VW Beetle.

"You don't have to…" I trail off as she walks away. I turn and face Spencer. "Hi."

"Hi."

I wait, hoping he'll say something to indicate Audrey's right. If he wants to get to know me, that would go a long way.

"Why won't you have dinner with me?" he demands.

My jaw drops.

He jams a hand in his hair. "I'm a chef. It's my thing. What's the problem, you don't like my cooking?"

"Your cooking is just fine."

"Then what?"

I park my hands on my hips. "I have to say I've never had such an angry dinner invitation before."

"I'm not angry. I'm frustrated."

I glance around. Just us here. I step closer and lower my voice. "Then why did you bail on me after we hooked up?"

His voice softens. "I left you a note."

"Because you couldn't face me in the morning."

He gestures toward the restaurant. "I had to get to work."

"Bullshit."

"Did you read the part where I said I hoped we could be friends? That meant I still wanted to see you."

I exhale sharply. *Friend zone.* Just what a woman wants to hear after great sex. Maybe he didn't think it was great.

I scowl at him.

He lifts his palms. "Your eyes were all teary and vulnerable over your ex, and I couldn't deal with tears over something I did." He exhales sharply. "I should've stayed and taken my punishment."

"Punishment?"

"Feeling wretched for causing you pain. I'm sorry I left. I should've just, I dunno, comforted you or something. If it helps, I felt wretched anyway."

He couldn't bear to cause me pain. I blink a few times. He's surprisingly sensitive, so worried over my hurt feelings that he apologized and took himself out of the picture. My eyes only welled because I felt so much for him in that moment. Halfway in love.

"And then I didn't hear from you for a week," I say. "Not cool."

"I was hoping with time things would smooth over, and we could be friends again." He looks to the sky. "It sounds stupid when I say it out loud."

"It was stupid. You don't ghost someone after a hookup. That's a no-second-chances scenario."

He runs a hand through his hair. "Guess you figured out I'm not great at relationships. I want to be better. With you, anyway."

I swallow over the lump of emotion lodged in my throat. He's being sincere. "I wasn't teary because of any vulnerability over my ex."

"So it was because of me?"

I look at a point just over his shoulder, not ready to explain how deep my feelings go for him. It's too soon, too new, and I'm not sure he's where I'm at. "I was just worn out. It wasn't about you or him. My day just caught up to me."

He pinches my chin, holding my gaze. "Be honest."

Looking into his eyes, that deep connection returns, warming me. I want to give him another chance, with more caution this time. "I'll have dinner with you at my place. You can cook in the inn's kitchen."

His hand shifts, cradling my jaw. "When?"

I swallow hard, nerves running through me. "Tomorrow works."

He flashes a smile and backs up a step, bouncing a little. "Okay. Great. I'm already coming up with the menu. For Bear too."

I can't help my smile. "Sounds good."

He points at me. "It'll be great. Count on that."

My smile widens. He apologized sincerely. And any guy who takes pains to include my dog in dinner plans deserves a second chance.

Here I am on my first real date with Spencer. So far it doesn't feel so different from when he's usually cooking in the inn's kitchen. We have guests at the inn, but they're out at the moment. Spencer gave them all free appetizers at The Horseman Inn to get rid of them. He was annoyed that I invited him over while I'm still technically working. I suppose I could've held off a few more days, but he was so eager to cook for me, and part of me couldn't wait.

He's making chicken cordon bleu, along with a thinly sliced potato au gratin and broccolini. Bear will enjoy a burger after our dinner. Spencer pops the potato dish into the oven. "Too bad you're working tonight."

I sip my wine. "You seemed really into cooking for me, so I agreed."

He shoots me a dark look. "Now you'll be distracted."

I gesture around the room. "Just us now."

"And Bear."

Bear's sound asleep against the back door, lying on his back with his little paws in the air. So cute with that furry golden belly exposed.

"I don't think he's going to give away your secrets," I say with a laugh.

"C'mere."

"Why?"

"Why're you so difficult?"

I raise my brows. "Excuse me?"

He jabs a hand in my direction. "You've been standing six feet away from me all night and with a counter between us."

I lean across the counter that separates the kitchen from the dining area, resting on my forearms. "I didn't want to get in your way."

He swaggers out of the kitchen, and I straighten, trying to remain unaffected by the sheer physicality of him. I've seen every sculpted muscle on that big body up close.

He steps into my personal space. I back up a step. His arm snakes around my waist, halting my retreat. My pulse skitters, my breath coming harder.

"That's better," he murmurs right before his lips meet mine. A rush of desire hits me just like the last time we kissed. *I missed this.* His fingers spear through my hair, holding me in place for a kiss that goes on and on. My knees go weak as my fingers clutch his shirt, desire pooling between my legs.

*Ruf! Ruf! Ruf!*

Spencer pulls back with a wry smile. "Bear wants in on the action."

He scoops up Bear, who's standing by my feet like a fierce protector, and holds him up to me so we're nose to nose. Bear tries to lick my mouth, but I shift, taking him and holding him close like my little baby with his front paws over my shoulder.

I stroke him behind the ears. "Get ready for burger." I turn to Spencer. He has a soft look in his eyes, tender almost, like he has some feeling for me. My stomach flutters, my pulse racing. "Everything smells so good."

He snaps to attention and goes back to the kitchen. "You're a distraction, Winters."

"So now we're on a last-name basis?"

"I only call my closest friends by their last name. Be glad you're worthy."

*Mixed signals much?* He kisses me and calls me his friend. No wonder I'm so confused where I stand with him.

"I'm so flattered." I set my wriggling puppy down, and he does a search for crumbs in the kitchen. "So we're close friends now."

"Yeah, the kissing kind."

"Is that like friends with benefits?"

"You tell me."

I busy myself setting the dining room table for us. Not going there. I'm in way too deep to pretend I can pull off a friends-with-benefits situation.

"Have you started looking for a new car?" he asks.

"Still waiting for the insurance money to come through."

"I can get you a deal. My dad owns a chain of car dealerships. Used and new, mostly Nissans, Chevys, and Jeeps with a few other models thrown in there."

"That would be great, thanks."

"No problem. Have you managed to get more positive reviews for the inn?"

"One more. The groom from another wedding left us a raving four star."

"A rave but only four stars? Why so stingy with the stars?"

"I don't know. I guess everyone has their own scale for what constitutes a five-star stay. He complimented the staff, the room, and the cooking."

"See, I'm your ace in the hole."

"Modesty isn't your strong suit."

"That's because modesty doesn't get you anywhere." He sets the stuffed chicken in a large glass dish and washes his hands. "Any more weddings booked?"

"No, but *Bride Special*—that's a major bridal magazine— said they'd be interested in covering one if we do, so that's good. Now if we could only find a couple willing to tie the knot here."

"What about the best man's travel magazine?"

I sigh. "Finally heard back from his editor at *Leisure Travel*. She said her content is fully booked for the year, and I should check back in December for next summer."

"Well, that's something at least."

I watch as he slices the broccolini in one quick movement and sets it on a steamer. I have no interest in cooking, but when he does it, there's something fascinating about the assured way he moves. I appreciate competence. In retrospect, I probably shouldn't have given him a hard time for all of his unscheduled menu changes for events. He knows what he's doing, and it's always for the best, which I will admit only with a knife to the throat. Or another bouquet of roses from him. I'm easy.

He leans back against the counter, a hint of a smile playing around his lips. "I can scrounge up a bride for your article. Guaranteed five-star review."

I'm almost afraid to ask. "Who?"

"You. We already played fake married. We could go through a fake wedding without a license, so it looks good but isn't real. Then I'll leave a rave review."

My mind flashes to Spencer in a tux, gazing into my eyes with that tender look he gave me as my fake husband. My mouth goes dry, every nerve ending on alert. "That's crazy."

"We were very convincing that night as a married couple, and we've already got our stories straight. *And* I still have the rings."

*Why did he keep the rings? What does that mean?*

I cross my arms, desperately trying to keep my distance. I'm not going through all this again with him. I'm the one who's going to get hurt. "I suppose you'd like a real honeymoon. That's the catch, right? Then you'll bail after."

His eyes are intent on mine. "Never again, promise. You'll have to kick me out of bed."

My pulse races at the thought of another night with him. A good night with a good morning after. A *great* night. "It's still a crazy idea to get fake married, even without a catch."

He moves toward me, a gleam in his eyes that makes me both excited and wary. "I'm the catch, Paige."

I sputter for a moment at the sheer arrogance.

He rushes me, grabbing me in a hug and chuckling low by my ear. I struggle for a moment, afraid he's laughing at me, but then he shocks me, whispering in my ear, "You're the real catch."

~

*Spencer*

Paige goes utterly still in my arms. "What did you say?" she asks my chest.

Welp, no denying it now. I want her in my bed; I want her in my kitchen; I want her in my life. I can't screw this up like every other relationship. I have to tread carefully.

I pull back enough to look at her and take a deep bracing breath. "You're an amazing woman. In case it's not clear, I'm crazy about you."

"You are?"

"No one's ever gotten under my skin the way you do. You're beautiful, smart, strong. The perfect complement to me."

"Maybe you're the perfect complement to me." A hint of a smile plays around her lips. "Because you're also beautiful, smart, and strong."

I drop my arms from her. "Yeah, okay. Why do I feel like I'm baring my soul and you're secretly laughing at me?"

She throws her arms around my neck and kisses me passionately. The fire ignites between us, all thoughts flying from my mind. I lift her to the island counter, our mouths fused. Her hands run all over me, her legs wrapping around my waist. Need like I've never known before roars through me.

She breaks the kiss. "Wait. Dinner."

I nearly groan. She's right. I can't let all this good food go to waste. The point of tonight was to show her my best qualities, though I'm no slouch in the bedroom. She's already had a taste of that.

I take a step back. "You're right."

"I love hearing you say I'm right. So sweet." She grabs my head and kisses me again. Then she pushes me away. "Go. Finish what you were doing."

"I was about to take you to bed. Should we finish that?"

She strokes my jaw. "You're back to scruff. I liked the beard."

"Noted." I take her hand from my jaw and kiss the palm. "Back to the kitchen for me. I promised you dinner."

She smiles, looking pleased, and all I want to do is please her more. I head back to the kitchen and finish preparing dinner. Paige takes Bear outside and gets some music going for us. A mellow mix of soft rock.

By the time we're seated at the dining room table, I'm past the sharp edge of lust, but not quite past the need. I'm not sure how long I can wait to be with her again. I remember every moment of our night together. Her sweet vanilla scent, satiny skin, her throaty sounds. I stifle a groan.

She cuts into the chicken cordon bleu. "Wow, this looks like what you'd get at a fancy restaurant."

"Spencer's. That's what I'm going to call my restaurant once I can afford my own place."

"Spencer's what?"

"Just Spencer's."

"Spencer's Place, Spencer's Bistro, Spencer's Grill?"

"People can decide what they want to think of it as. For me, it's going to be a farm-to-table restaurant on a property where I can grow fresh fruit and vegetables and keep some animals."

"A real working farm? You know how to do that?"

"I'll find people who do."

She takes a bite of chicken, and her eyes roll back in her head.

My gut tightens. I want her so frigging bad. It's not just the fact that she's sexy and loves food and my cooking, it's her. Fiery, sweet her.

"Omigod, Spencer, it's amazing. Try some."

My voice comes out hoarse. "I know what it tastes like. Thank you."

She takes another bite, her expression pure bliss.

I eat my dinner, watching her the whole time. She's so into

the food she doesn't pause for conversation. The ultimate compliment to the chef. The food entranced her.

She finishes, sets her fork down, and sighs. "I could get used to this."

"Me too. Seems we're perfectly compatible, so why did we fight so much before?"

She shakes her head. "I don't know. Your arrogance?"

"Hmm, maybe your hardheaded bossiness."

"Which you share."

I bite back a smile. "I know what the problem was. You got mad whenever I changed the menu or said anything remotely flirty."

Her whiskey eyes hold a touch of amusement. She enjoys our fights as much as I do, though now there's an undercurrent of warmth to them. "Yes, but now I see you know what you're doing in the kitchen, so I should've just let you run free."

"Fact. Big of you to admit it. Now why did you hate it when I flirted? Most women love that."

She looks to the ceiling before leveling her gaze on me. "Because it wasn't unique to *me*. You're flirty with everyone. You flirted with me and my sister at the same time at our first meeting at the inn."

"That's just how I am with women."

"News flash—a woman wants to feel like she's the only one getting special attention. I'll tell you right now I don't believe in seeing multiple people at the same time. If a person is interesting enough for me to date, that's the only person I want to date. And I expect the same from him."

*Perfect.* A woman who knows what she wants—me.

"Are we dating?" I ask.

Pink tinges her cheeks, and she fusses with her napkin, folding it and setting it on the table. "Tonight seemed like a first date."

"Technically, it's our second date, and I haven't seen anyone in between. Guess that makes you the only person I'm dating."

Her lips quirk to the side as she thinks about that. I sense an argument coming on, so I take that moment to get out the burger I prepared earlier and put a small amount in a bowl for Bear. He wolfs it down and licks his chops.

Paige joins me in the kitchen with the dishes, rinsing them and putting them in the dishwasher. She finishes and turns to me. "The thing is, I don't want to be the default only person you're dating. I want you to choose that. No wishy-washy—" she lowers her voice to a deep tone, doing a terrible impersonation of me "—guess that makes you the only person I'm dating. Have you ever been monogamous?"

I let out an exaggerated sigh, pretending offense. "See, you judged me by my flirtiness, assuming that meant I was a player."

She fusses with her hair, smoothing it back. "Well…"

"That's just harmless fun. I'm always monogamous, which is probably why nothing lasts long. Once I lose interest, I end it with a clean break and move on to the next person. Only a coward cheats. As I seem to remember telling you before. I don't mind repeating it, given your poor experience with a lesser man."

She smiles widely, her eyes warm. She likes the implication that I'm calling her ex a coward. It's the truth anyway.

I ramble on, hoping I'm getting this right. "I guess I have to take some responsibility for the shortness of my relationships. If I were better at them, it seems like something would've stuck by now. I want things to be different with you."

She sighs. I'm not sure if that's a good or bad sign.

"You want me," I say, daring her to deny it.

She throws her hands in the air. "You drive me crazy."

I close the distance, banding an arm around her waist and stroking a finger down the side of her neck. "But in the *you're crazy about me* way."

Her eyes flash, her palms pressed flat against my chest. "We're not going to bed together tonight. This was just dinner."

"How about the kitchen?" I lean down, kissing along her neck, letting my teeth scrape against her. She shivers.

"My guests are coming back any minute," she whispers.

"They can let themselves in."

She looks toward the front door.

"Let me in," I say against her lips.

She pulls back to look at me. "I don't know if you mean that in the dirty way or the getting-to-know-you way."

"Both."

She grabs my head and speaks in a fierce tone. "Don't make me regret this."

"Do you regret the first time?"

"Yes!"

"Why?"

"Because you left me a goddamn note apologizing, bailed, and ghosted me for a week, that's why."

"This time you'll have to kick me out of bed." I kiss her, but she pulls away, searching my expression.

A crackling moment of tension passes between us, our gazes locked. Didn't I tell her I'm crazy about her? She's crazy about me too. She admitted it. Kinda.

I'm not about to beg. That's the move of a desperate man. She has to meet me halfway.

"Please." I draw her back to me and kiss her again, deepening the kiss. She softens against me, her arms wrapping around me. *Yes! Mine, all mine.*

Bear barks.

She pulls away, smiling. "Bear wants me all to himself."

"He'll have to fight me for the privilege." I scoop her up in my arms and carry her through the inn and up the stairs to her apartment.

## 12

*Paige*

Spencer halts at the entrance to my bedroom, setting me back on my feet. "So this is the inner sanctum. I expected more pink."

I glance at my queen-sized bed with its white comforter and beige upholstered headboard. The walls are a light brown; the ceiling white. "There's some pink in the area rug."

"Mostly beige. This is a place a guy could get comfortable."

Before I can figure out how to respond to that, his lips meet mine, his hands sliding under my silk blouse, roaming up my sides. A blaze of heat flashes through me in an instant. I tug on his shirt, yanking it from the waistband of his jeans.

He moves faster, stripping me out of my things as he kisses me, and then he's guiding me toward the bed. The backs of my knees hit the mattress, and he pushes me back. I'm naked, and he's only shirtless.

I prop up on my elbows, about to demand he strip, when he spreads my legs. He kneels between them and kisses up the inside of one leg. I drop back weakly, sensation racing through me.

He kisses his way up the inside of my other leg, reaches damn close to where I want him, pauses, and looks at me.

"You gave me a second chance. I believe in rewarding that."
He dips his head, dropping a kiss on my sex. *Yes!* Desire
pulses through me. I remember how good he is at this. I'm
nearly vibrating in anticipation.

He spreads me wide with his fingers, his tongue doing
wicked things. I throw my arms to my sides, lost in pleasure.

My hips rock mindlessly as he pushes me closer and closer
to the edge. *Oh God.*

The phone on the nightstand rings—my work phone for
the inn—and my head whips toward it. The guests at the inn
probably need something.

One big hand clamps on my hip, holding me in place.

"I have to get that," I say.

He lifts his head. "You have to come for me first."

"Spence—ah!" The intensity skyrockets as he pins me in
place with both hands on my hips, pushing me relentlessly
on. And then he sucks gently, and I explode with a harsh
cry. White-hot pleasure fires through me, all the way to my
toes.

I go limp in a dazed state of wonder, staring blankly at the
ceiling.

He shifts away from the bed. I hear the rustle of clothes,
the rip of a condom wrapper.

I'm suddenly aware the phone's ringing again. I scramble
to my knees, crawling over to it on the nightstand. I grab it
just as Spencer grabs me from behind, covering me with the
heat of his body.

"Hello," I say, out of breath.

"Can we get an extra pillow in the green room?" an older
woman asks. Dorothy, I think.

Spencer bites along the side of my neck hard enough to
sting. I hold back a gasp.

"Yes!" I say. "Happy to get that over to you."

"Thank you, dear. I need it for my hips."

Spencer aligns our bodies, and I try to get her off the
phone quickly. "No problem! I'm in the middle of something
for another guest, and I'll be there. Give me twenty minutes."
A sudden thrust steals my breath as he fills me.

Spencer's deep voice vibrates in my ear. "I need more than twenty."

The woman continues. "The doctor says it helps keep them in alignment."

"More than twenty," I manage.

"Harold, do you need anything?" she asks her husband.

Spencer's fingers stroke gently between my legs as he thrusts deep. I whimper softly.

"Are you okay, honey?" the clueless woman asks.

"Yes," I say hoarsely.

"Harold would like some extra washcloths."

Spencer thrusts again, sending a rush of pleasure through me.

"Yes, yes," I say. "Everything you need. Twenty, thirty minutes." I hang up and drop the phone on the nightstand with a clatter. Then I smack Spencer over my shoulder. "You're going to get me another bad review."

"I expect five stars from you. Now be a good girl and take it."

His teeth clamp on the cord of my neck as he rocks into me, one deep thrust after another. He's relentless, pushing me higher and higher. His fingers join in the action—stroking, teasing, circling. The primal hold, his heat at my back, the feeling of complete possession takes me to a place of blissful surrender. I tremble under him, and he whispers praise in my ear.

It's too much suddenly, my hips buck wildly, seeking release. He takes over, holding me still as he pumps slow and deep, his fingers grazing me lightly, driving me crazy.

I'm burning up. "Please, please."

His fingers leave me, and I protest the loss instantly. "Hey!"

He pushes my head down to the pillow, grabs my hips, and thrusts hard and fast. The angle hits in just the right spot. My insides coil hot and tight. I'm panting, pleasure spiraling deep within me.

He groans low, slowing it down again.

I whimper incoherently, beyond speech as I silently beg

for more. He keeps me there, hovering near the knife edge of release with his slow, deep thrusts.

He covers me, speaking near my ear. "You're going to come for me now, beautiful."

A shiver ripples through me in anticipation. "Yes," I manage.

His fingers are back, stroking me with just the right pressure as he rocks into me, stroking on the inside at the same time. It builds inside me, an intense climb. The sound of his harsh breath reaches me. He wants my pleasure; he's holding back for me. *Love.*

My hips buck once, twice, and he holds me tight to him, his fingers working me. *Fire, I'm on fire.* I cry out, the orgasm hitting hard, rocketing through me with shocking intensity.

He clamps my hips in his large hands, pulling me back onto him with each hard thrust. I pant harshly, every movement bringing more pleasure. He lets out a guttural groan, clasping me tight to him as he finally lets go. I feel him throb inside me, my own throbbing a constant pulse.

When he finally releases me, I collapse to the mattress, spent. He lands next to me, flopping onto his back.

He brushes my hair back from my face. "No regrets, Paige."

It sounds like a bossy order, but I like it. "No regrets."

He kisses my temple and the corner of my mouth. I smile sleepily.

I'm not sure how much time passes, but I wake in the dark when I hear Spencer moving around. Dammit! Is he bailing again?

"Where are you going?" I demand. He said no regrets. He said I'd have to kick him out of bed this time, which I did *not.*

He crawls back into bed, fully dressed, and covers me with his body, propping himself on his forearms. "You mean where have I been, Sleeping Beauty? While you were snoring—"

"I don't snore."

"Making a low roar," he amends. "I delivered the towels

and extra pillow to your guests and let Bear out for a walk before putting him in his crate."

I stare at the ceiling in the dark. "I can't believe I forgot to do that stuff. That could've been bad in so many ways."

"I distracted you, so it was on me."

I wrap my arms around his neck. "True. I was involuntarily having phone sex with an older woman on the line."

He chuckles. "I could hear both parts of the conversation." His fingers stroke down my throat. "But you were too sexy to resist."

"How'd you know where to find the towels and extra pillow?"

"I got them from your bathroom closet."

"Those are mine! The stuff for the guests is in the laundry room downstairs."

He kisses me long and deep. "Can't have you mad at me at a time like this."

He kisses his way down my body, and I sigh and then gasp.

∿

*Spencer*

Now I'm really regretting leaving Paige the morning after our first time together because this Paige is soft and cuddly. Who knew?

It's early. She has to cook the guests' breakfast in a bit. I'm going to do it for her because I'm just that awesome.

She's curled on her side, plastered against me, her head on my shoulder, her hand roaming over my bare chest. "You've been a surprise, Spencer Wolf."

"Which part?"

"All of it. I thought you were so arrogant and not at all my type."

"One, it's called confidence. Two, what's your type?"

"Someone who likes conversation—"

"Long walks on the beach—"

"Oh, sorry, do you already know my type?"

"I know what you *think* you want. It's the standard request on every dating site. But what you really want is me."

She kisses my neck. "You did me a huge favor stepping in as my wedding date. I owe you one."

I arch my brows. "Yeah? What do I get?"

She sits up. "I'm going to find you the perfect location for Spencer's."

"There's some farm property upstate I've been eyeing. More than one place, actually, near where I grew up."

"Did you grow up on a farm?"

"No, but there was farmland around us. I loved getting fresh fruit and vegetables from the farmers' market with my mom on the weekends. It started my journey to food."

"How far upstate?"

"An hour north of here."

"Oh." Her expression dims. She doesn't want me to move even an hour away. Who knew Paige had a sweet side?

She props up on her elbow, and the blanket shifts off her, giving me a nice view of her plump breasts. "Have you considered looking around here?"

"Too expensive."

"Where do you live now?"

"I rent a lakeside house from a couple. It's their second home, and they've been busy with their grandchildren in Virginia, so they rented it out. It's small—three bedrooms, two baths—but it's in good condition."

"That's not small. Did you grow up in a mansion or something?"

"Not a mansion, exactly. A mini-mansion. I told you my dad owns a chain of car dealerships."

"Why don't you ask him for a loan for your restaurant?"

*Right.* Dad's so pissed I didn't join him in the family business he barely speaks to me. It's only Mom who keeps the peace between us when we get together on holidays.

I glance at the clock. "Almost time for your guests' breakfast. I'd better get dressed."

She grabs my arm. "You don't have to leave."

I cup the back of her neck and pull her close for a kiss.

"I'm going to make breakfast. It's my recipes you're using, after all."

She launches herself at me, surprising me with the move. I fall to my back with her on top. She kisses me all over my face.

I smile widely. She's definitely crazy about me.

≈

*Paige*

I practically float out the door when I take Bear for his early morning walk. I think I'm in love with Spencer. It makes me giddy and squirmy at the same time. Like it's almost too good to be true. I'm still trying to reconcile the irritating, arrogant persona with the wonderful side he's shown me. He's generous in and out of the bedroom, which is a rare quality in a guy. Okay, so he's bossy, but that can be sexy. I flush with heat remembering last night. I don't mind him bossing in the bedroom because everything he does is for my pleasure.

He's ambitious and hardworking like me. And he cooks! Does it get any better than that?

After my walk with Bear, I head to the kitchen. Spencer's already there with a basket of herbs and vegetables that look like they were just picked from our garden. Most of that stuff was planted under his direction. The guests are still sleeping.

"Have a seat and watch the master," he says.

"Gladly." Any day off from cooking is a good day.

He pulls eggs from the refrigerator. "When does Brooke take over?"

"She'll be here by four today and take the Sunday morning breakfast shift tomorrow."

"I'm working tonight until ten. You want to come over to my place after? I don't have to be back at work until eleven on Sunday."

I rock my head side to side. "Depends. Is this a booty call?"

He crosses to me, backing me up against the counter, his hands on either side of my body. He leans close, his words hot against my ear. "Do you need a booty call? I thought I left you more than satisfied."

"Hmm, it's all a little fuzzy in my mind."

He nips my neck. "I'll remind you."

"You must be early birds like me and Harold!" a chirpy voice exclaims.

I whirl to face my guest Dorothy, and Spencer gives my butt a pat, surprising me. I keep a straight face despite the heat in my cheeks. "Good morning. We're just getting breakfast started. Can I get you coffee or tea?"

Dorothy smiles, her face full of smile lines. Her hair is blondish-white in a short bob. "Two teas, please. Harold and I are going to check out the wedding pergola. We didn't realize you did elopements here. We eloped fifty years ago. Might be nice to do it again!"

"We'd be happy to arrange a vow renewal," I say.

Harold, a tall thin man with a full head of gray hair, smiles and takes her hand, entwining their fingers together. He lifts her hand and kisses her knuckles.

"Such a charmer," she coos.

They head out the back door to the yard, speaking in low tones to each other.

I turn to Spencer. "Can you not touch my ass in front of the guests?"

He cracks two eggs with one hand into a bowl and leers at me. "Where do we stand on the other erogenous zones?"

I shake my head. "Phone sex was bad enough."

He washes his hands, dries them, and turns to face me. "That wasn't phone sex. That was actual sex with an unsuspecting witness."

"Shh! There are other guests here."

"C'mere, gimme some sugar."

"Get it yourself."

He lunges for me, and I squeak, turn, and race out of the room. He chases me, catching me easily and wrapping his arms around me from behind. It feels so nice to be held I don't fight it.

He nuzzles into my neck, his scruff rubbing deliciously against me. "You're a lot more fun than I suspected."

"I'm not even going to ask what that means."

"You were so witchy before."

I stiffen. "Thanks. Good to know."

"You must've enchanted me."

I have no idea what to say to that, but I don't need to speak. He kisses a hot trail along my neck, and I sink against him.

I fear I'm the one who's enchanted.

## 13

*Spencer*

I'm off work today since The Horseman Inn is closed on Mondays, and Paige has time off since her last guests checked out this morning. It's the last week of August, a gorgeous summer day, so we're driving to look at a property a couple of hours away. The one I had my eye on before already sold. Paige found this place closer to my price range, but farther away from her than I wanted.

It's been two awesome weeks with Paige. I don't know why we work, but we do. We're like a power team, having each other's backs. I even like her dog, which is good because she always has him close. Except for today's outing she left Bear at her brother Wyatt's house for a doggie playdate.

I park my truck and pull into the gravel driveway of the property. There's lots of land with trees farther in the distance. The house is an old white clapboard, nothing special. There's a gray-sided barn and a few outbuildings.

Paige hops out of the truck and heads for the house. I follow, trying to imagine this place as a destination restaurant.

Paige unlocks the front door. She has the keys from the realty office. The family that lives here went out so we could check it out on our own. The wooden door creaks open.

"Ready?" she asks.

"This place is more isolated than I thought."

"It's ten minutes to the downtown."

"Which is one street."

"Not so different from Summerdale." She steps inside.

I follow. "It's a lot different from Summerdale. First, there's not a lot of houses around here. I need population density to support a restaurant."

"Nice staircase," she says, pointing to the newel post and the polished oak rail.

I glance around. Scuffed hardwood floors, a fireplace in the living room, a worn sofa with too many throw pillows. Everything about this feels wrong.

"Let's check out the kitchen," she says.

I follow her to a kitchen with oak cabinets and laminate counters. Four-burner electric stove. Not gonna cut it. I hate the blue and green striped wallpaper.

"This house needs a lot of work," I say.

"If you want to convert it to a restaurant, then yes. Or you could convert the barn into a restaurant."

"It's too small."

She gives me a tight smile. "You knew the dimensions before we showed up here."

"It's ugly."

She sighs. "You could build a new structure on the property with a similar architectural style to the house."

I jam a hand through my hair. "This place seemed good on paper, but now I'm not sure."

She ticks off my list. "Lots of land, house, outbuildings, upstate New York."

"It's *too* upstate."

"I don't know what that means."

"It's two hours from Summerdale."

I turn and walk out of the room, feigning interest in the rest of the downstairs. I almost said *it's two hours from you*. I can't base my future life decisions on our relationship. We've only been seeing each other for a month. So what if I'm halfway in love with her? She hasn't said the same. Just because she's soft and cuddly after sex doesn't mean she's where I'm at. I swear she loves her dog more than me sometimes. Always cooing over Bear and holding him close.

My shoulders droop. *Am I seriously jealous of a dog?*

I don't like this love feeling, if that's what this is. Everything feels charged and slightly out of control. Paige never even fights with me anymore, which at least let me relax, like we were playing a game. I care too much. For the first time I don't want to walk away, and if she walks away from me, she's going to inflict serious damage. Vulnerable is not in my comfort zone.

She catches up to me in the dining room. "It's the only place that has everything you want in your price range."

I press my lips together. "Then I'll just have to save more money."

"Okay, so should I look for property in Summerdale? It seems like you're maybe a little more attached to your adopted town than I thought."

*I'm attached to you.*

"Aren't you?"

"Sure. I'm personally invested in the inn. It's my home and my business. I'm not going anywhere, but you're renting, and this is your dream." She spreads her arms wide. "Spencer's."

"It sucks."

"Oh-kay, onward. I'll find you the perfect match, don't worry. I know my way around real estate."

She strides cheerfully past me, and I grab her arm, halting her. She looks up at me, a question in her eyes.

I'm the one with questions. "Why don't you fight with me anymore? I'm being very difficult."

She peels my hand off her arm. "I've yet to find an easy client."

"So now I'm just a client?"

She pats my shoulder. "One of many titles. We should go and let the family know you're not interested."

"You were more fun when you got mad all the time."

She ignores me, walking out of the house. I find her on the porch, waiting to lock up, calm as can be.

"You don't even care that I could move two hours away," I say.

She locks the door and turns to me. "Would you like me to throw a fit and insist you give up your dream and stay for my sake?"

My lips twitch. It does sound kinda ridiculous when she says it like that. "Okay, let me put it this way, *I* don't want to be two hours away from you. Our lives will get busy, the visits will get farther apart, until it's too much, and then whatever this *thing* is between us, this connection, will break."

*I think I'm in love with you.*

*Don't say it.*

She takes my hand, still looking cheerful as she walks with me to the truck. "And you don't want our connection to break."

"No, do you?"

"No, but I want you to have your dream restaurant. And if that has to happen here where you can afford it, then that's what has to happen. We can still visit each other."

"Didn't you hear the part about the distance? Say we both have off on a Monday. You want to spend four hours of your only day off commuting to see me?"

"Or you could commute to me."

"I'll be too busy farming and renovating. I won't be able to afford much help until the restaurant opens."

She taps her finger against her lips. "Hmm...so you're saying we'll have to decide if we hook up during our visit or just sit around watching the vegetables grow, Farmer Wolf? Not such a good name for a farmer, you'll scare away the chickens."

She's teasing me. I'm about to get defensive when it occurs to me that she may have brought me here just to show me this isn't what I want. That means she wants me closer to her.

I grab her in a hug, and she squeaks in surprise.

I kiss her temple. "You're still not used to my sudden hugs."

"If I knew you were being affectionate, I wouldn't be startled, but they seem to come out of nowhere. I haven't figured out what's going on in that head of yours."

I close my eyes, relaxing with her back in my arms. "That's okay. I know what's in yours."

She pulls back to look at me. "Do you?"

"Yeah, beautiful, you don't want me to live two hours away. You brought me here to show me how awful it is."

"Is that right?"

"You want me close by just as much as Bear."

She laughs and kisses me. "I'm not sure I want to know what's going on in that head of yours."

I backpedal, fearing I revealed too much. "I'm not jealous of Bear."

"Okay," she says, laughing. "We'd better get back to my true love."

She gets in the truck, and I join her, leaning over to kiss her. "You already found him."

She shoves my chest playfully. "I can't believe you're jealous of a dog."

My heart kicks harder as I admit the truth. "I've never felt like this before."

She blinks rapidly, her eyes welling. "Oh, Spencer."

My heart lurches at the sight of her tears, and I pull her into my arms. "Don't cry. It's an uncomfortable feeling, but I'll get used to it."

She cups my jaw, smiling through tears. I press her head to my chest, trying to protect her from whatever caused her tears. I said something wrong, but I'm not sure what.

"Why exactly are you crying?" I ask.

She straightens. "Because I'm happy. You just told me how much I mean to you."

I grunt. I didn't say that exactly, but it's spooky how she read my mind just then.

She kisses my neck, shifting to straddle me. I glance

around as lust roars through me. Still looking isolated out here. Not a single car on the road.

She kisses me roughly, and there's no going back. I'm rock hard. She undoes the button and zipper on my jeans. I slide a hand under her silky summer dress, find her damp through her panties, and groan. I shift them to the side, and she takes me in hand, guiding me inside, her eyes locked on mine. Raw emotion takes me by surprise, lodging a lump in my throat. Our joining is more than just physical.

A charged moment passes between us. *Love.*

And then she rocks against me fast, and there's nothing but primal need. Within minutes, we're both panting. I slide my hand between us, strumming on the spot that makes her crazy.

She gasps, riding faster, her head thrown back in ecstasy. She goes off, taking me with her as her body contracts around me. I hold her tight, keeping us joined.

Still panting, she lifts her head. "We should get going. Don't want to get caught like this."

"I love this feeling, buried deep inside you." I throb, and she gasps.

Her eyes widen. "We forgot the condom."

"I'm healthy."

"So am I, but I'd rather not be pregnant without a husband."

"I'll marry you." I've never said that in my life, but in that moment, I mean it. I want to marry her.

She climbs off me and adjusts her clothes. "That's not a reason to get married. Don't worry about it."

"I'm not worried."

"Well, I am!"

She's fighting with me again. Pure joy fires through me. It's time to tell her how it's going to be because this is real. "Our baby would be very much wanted. You'll make a great mom. I've seen you with Bear."

She launches herself at me, kissing all over my face. Heat radiates through my chest as Paige loves on me. I can't stop touching her, stroking her hair, her back, everywhere I can reach.

She smiles and returns to her seat, putting her seatbelt on. I start the truck.

She bites her lower lip. "I am thirty. It's not like I have a lot of time to wait on kids."

I grin. "I'm twenty-nine. If this time wasn't a direct hit, maybe we should wait until I have mature thirty-year-old swimmers."

She laughs. "Don't think that matters in the grand scheme of things."

My phone rings. I find it on the side of the seat where it must've fallen out during our spontaneous truck hookup. "It's my mom," I tell Paige.

"I should meet her."

"She'd be in shock. I've never brought a woman home to meet my parents before." I answer the phone. "Hi, Mom. How's it going?"

"Spencer…" Her voice sounds frail and far away. Adrenaline fires through me.

"What is it? What's wrong?"

Her voice comes out so soft I have to press the phone closer to my ear. "It was so sudden. Your dad, he's dead."

I drop the phone, and it clatters to the floor. My vision blurs as I stare blankly out the windshield.

Paige presses the phone back in my hand. "What's wrong?"

I put the phone back to my ear. "What happened?"

"Heart attack." Mom's voice cracks. "Can you come home?"

"Yes, I'm about an hour away. Hang on, I'll be there soon." I hang up, my gut churning.

"Spencer?"

I stare numbly out the windshield. "My dad died."

"Oh, I'm so sorry."

"I have to go home." I can't seem to move.

"Let me drive. Just give me the address."

I step out of the truck and promptly throw up. Paige's arm

goes around my shoulders. "Okay, it's going to be okay. I'm here with you." She gets tissues from her purse for me to clean up and fetches her water from the truck.

I clean up as best I can. Paige takes care of everything and then takes my hand, pulling me to the other side of the truck.

Somehow I get into the passenger side. Paige shuts the door behind me and makes her way to the driver's seat. She pulls up the GPS and finds my parents' address programmed in there.

She backs out and heads down the street.

"Looks like you're going to meet my mom after all," I say.

"This is *not* how I wanted it to happen, but I'll do whatever needs doing for both of you, okay? You just be with her. You'll need each other right now. My dad died from a heart attack very suddenly—"

"Mine too."

She takes my hand in a tight clasp. It's the only thing that feels real right now.

## 14

_Paige_

I've never seen Spencer like this. I think he's in shock. He's barely spoken two words to me in a week. Now we're at his mom's house for a funeral reception with family and friends. There's a good turnout of people. Spencer's mom, Olivia, is a sweet gentle woman. Spencer says he took after his dad in personality—headstrong and determined. His mom was always the peacemaker between them.

The reception seems to go on forever, and I can tell it's become a strain on Spencer. "You want me to clear people out?" I ask him.

"No, Mom needs them around her. Let's take a walk."

"Sure." I follow him out through the garage to avoid running into too many people. We pass a '57 Chevy raised up on jacks with no tires.

"Dad's baby," Spencer says, tapping the hood as we pass. "He loved cars. This one was a work in progress since I was in high school. I worked on it a bit with him until I took a different path."

"Do you want it?"

"No. Cars aren't my thing. I only know the basics anyway. Not like him."

We step outside, and he taps a keypad to close the garage

door behind us. I follow him down the winding road dotted with houses. He grew up in a beautiful area with lots of trees and well-kept yards. "So this is Spencer country. Now I understand the kind of town you want to establish your restaurant in with lots of open space for your farm."

"That's the plan." He takes my hand as we walk down the street. "Mom looks numb."

"She's probably in shock. I get the feeling you are too. You've barely spoken at all since you heard. Understandable, it was sudden."

He blows out a breath. "I've been thinking a lot about Dad and the fights we used to have. He thought I was turning my back on family by not joining him in the business. He ran the empire. Then it was supposed to go to me so he could gradually step back, knowing his legacy was protected."

"That's a lot of pressure on an only child. If you had a brother or sister, they could've stepped up. Maybe for someone else it would've been a good fit, but, Spencer, I've watched you in the kitchen. It's so clear that's where you're happiest. And you're a fantastic chef. You took the path you were meant to take in life."

"Part of me knows that, and part of me can't shake the guilt that if I'd taken some of the burden off him, he'd still be here today." His voice cracks. "Mom told me the doctor said his stress level was too high. He was stretched too thin." He turns to me, pain in his eyes. "Paige, he needed me."

My heart lurches at his pain. "Sometimes the doctors don't even know what causes a heart attack. There could've been another issue with his heart."

"It was me."

I stop short and cup his face in my hands. "Listen to me, Spencer. It's *not* your fault."

He's quiet, his jaw tight.

"If he needed help, he could've hired someone qualified to join him."

He gives me a quick hug, takes my hand, and continues our walk. "That wouldn't have worked. He couldn't have bossed them the way he could family."

"You hate being bossed. You *are* the boss."

He looks to the sky. "Finally, you've seen the light." He gives me a wry look. "This is why we fought before, because you mistakenly thought you could boss me."

I relax a little, hearing him sound more like himself. "In that case, I *was* the boss. I hired you for a job; therefore, I'm the boss of everyone I hired."

"With me as the exception."

I shake my head. "I'm not arguing with you right now, just know I agree to disagree."

A black SUV drives up behind us and pulls to a stop. The window powers down, and a woman in her sixties looks out at us. "Bye, Spencer. Sorry again for your loss. Cal was a good man." She smiles at me. "Nice to meet you."

Spencer lifts a hand. "Thanks, Mrs. Wain. I appreciate it."

"Nice to meet you too," I say.

She gestures back toward the house. "Your mom's getting tired, so we're clearing out to give her a chance to rest. I'm organizing a meal chain. She'll have a fresh dinner dropped off every day for the next two weeks."

"We both appreciate it."

She gives him a sympathetic smile. "Take care."

We turn back toward the house, and another car stops, the driver leaning out to express their condolences. After the third car, Spencer strides quickly toward the house, steering me to the edge of the street and giving quick waves to people on their way out. We go through the side yard, bypassing the house, and go to the backyard, where he guides me to a free-standing porch swing with an awning over it for shade.

"I'm going to wait them out," he says. "I can't take another 'sorry for your loss.'"

"I get it. People don't know what to say. I remember being so angry at my dad's funeral. That phrase sounded trite to my kid ears. I wanted someone to say how unfair it was that he died young and that it never should've happened."

"How old were you?"

"Eleven."

He gives my hand a squeeze. "Too young to lose your

dad. Here I am, a full-grown adult with plenty of opportunities to visit or call, but I didn't. I showed up for holidays out of obligation."

I press against his side, trying to give him comfort.

He wraps his arm around my shoulders, keeping me close. "We had a strained relationship since I left home at eighteen. I could never be what he wanted, and every time I tried to share what I was doing or where I was working, he took it like a slap in the face. Like I was bragging about how great my life was compared to the life he could've given me."

"So sorry. If you're as much alike as you say, he must've given you a tough fight. Two hardheaded alphas butting heads."

He kisses the top of my head. "He did."

We sit quietly in the waning heat of August, idly swinging together.

Olivia, Spencer's mom, pokes her head out the patio door. She's a petite woman with shoulder-length blond hair. "Spencer, could you help with cleanup? Everyone's left."

He halts the swing. "Coming."

He stands, and I join him. "I'll help."

He puts his hands on my shoulders, his eyes intent on mine. "You've already helped more than you know just by being here."

"Of course. I'm probably the only one who has this same experience. I can relate."

He inclines his head. We start walking toward the house.

"Plus I love you," I say softly.

He halts. "What was that?"

I take a deep breath, gazing into his eyes. "I love you."

He closes his eyes for a moment.

"Too soon?"

He opens his eyes. "It's a relief because I've been in love with you since we met."

Pure happiness bubbles up within me. "You have not. You didn't even like me when we met, and I certainly didn't like you."

He holds up a finger. "Amendment. Since we met naked."

"Now that I believe."

He kisses me, and we walk back inside, holding hands. I've never felt closer to another person.

*Spencer*

With Paige's help, the house is cleaned up in no time. Now we're sitting in the living room with Mom. Paige and I are on a light gray upholstered sofa together. Mom's sitting on a light blue Louis XV-style armchair with a cup of tea she doctored with brandy. Mom did the whole house in French country style, which means soft fabric colors, lots of wood and natural materials, and vintage stuff. Dad's dark brown leather recliner stands in stark contrast, clashing with Mom's interior design. He loved that thing.

Mom catches me looking at it. "Would you like the recliner?"

"No, that's his."

"Well, obviously it's not going to get much use here."

"I'm sure you can find someone else who wants it."

Paige pipes up, "If you need help finding a home for certain things, I'm happy to help. I can call relatives or post online for a sale or just arrange a donation."

Mom gives her a soft smile. "I'm so glad Spencer finally settled down with a nice woman." She shoots me a dark look. "Took you long enough." Guess the brandy's kicking in because Mom is normally sweetness and light. Of course, this is a difficult time. My parents were close. They were opposites in personality, but that seemed to be part of what made them work. They appreciated what the other person brought to the table.

I give Paige a sideways glance. We're more similar than not, though I'll admit Paige has a sweet and loving side I never expected. I'm in love with this woman. It sorta snuck up on me. And she loves me back. A ray of light during this dark time.

An awkward silence falls.

"Excuse me, I'm going to use the powder room," Paige says.

As soon as she leaves, I lean forward, elbows on my knees. "Are you okay?"

"No, but I will be." Mom sighs, staring at the floor. "Eventually. You know the last thing Dad said to me?"

"What?"

She meets my eyes. "He said he wished he'd found someone high level to help him manage the business."

A stab of guilt hits, my chest tightening. That's the last thing he thought about—protecting his legacy with the business. I know and Mom knows that should've been me working at his side, taking the burden from his shoulders. Maybe Dad was thinking of me when he said it, wishing I'd stepped up. Regret and disappointment over his son until the last moment.

I blink back tears. There's nothing I can do now. No amount of visits or apologies or attempts at reconciliation can make one bit of difference. He's gone.

"Did he even try to find someone?" I finally ask.

She finishes her tea and sets the cup on a coaster on the wooden coffee table. "He tried, but he couldn't find anyone he liked. He said he needed another one of him."

Bile rises in my throat, my gut churning. That would be me. Even Dad acknowledged how similar we were. Mom blames me for not stepping up too. Except selling cars was never my goal. I don't know what to say. Sorry doesn't cut it.

Mom gives me a watery smile. "So now you'll finally be taking on the family business like Dad always wanted."

I stare at her, confused. "What makes you say that?"

"He left it all to you."

I jackknife upright in my seat, my head rearing back. "Why would he do that? What about you?"

"He provided enough for me with his life insurance policy. The business was always meant for you."

I stand abruptly. "Well, I don't want it. I'll sign it over to you."

"Spencer, you can't go against your father's wishes."

My guilt morphs into anger. "The hell I can't. He's forcing me into a position I never wanted." This is the ultimate revenge from Dad. He's probably gloating in heaven.

Paige walks in. "Everything okay?"

"No," I snap. "We're going."

Mom frowns. "Spencer Ian Wolf, sit down."

Twenty-nine and I'm getting the full-name treatment. I take my seat, mostly because I don't want to upset her more than she already is over losing Dad.

Paige stands on the far side of the room, looking uncertain.

I gesture her over.

Mom turns. "Please join us, Paige. We're just discussing Spencer's inheritance."

Paige quickly returns to my side on the sofa, taking my hand and giving it a squeeze.

Mom continues in her soothing, conciliatory voice, just like when she used to try to make peace between me and Dad. Even now, she's the peacemaker. "Dad isn't forcing your hand. He loved you very much. This is his last gift to you."

Paige's brows rise in question.

I fill Paige in. "Dad left me the car dealerships. Five of them."

"Oh wow," Paige says. "You'd finally have enough money for your restaurant."

"He can't sell!" Mom exclaims. "Spencer, you know that's not what Dad would've wanted."

I speak through my teeth, trying to rein in my temper. "Dad knew I didn't want this. This is his last-ditch effort to force me into it."

"Spencer." Mom's face crumples, and she rushes from the room.

I stand, going after her. "Mom."

She waves me away. "No. I need to be alone."

She goes upstairs.

I look at Paige, my lips pressed tightly together.

"Should we go?" she asks.

I nod, and we head out the door.

It never occurred to me to sell, but Paige is right. I'd be set for my dream restaurant. But at what price? I don't want to hurt Mom or cause bad blood between us. She might even disown me. I can't lose both of them.

∼

Three days later, I'm preparing an end-of-summer feast for the guests of The Inn on Lovers' Lane. I haven't been myself. I suppose that's to be expected with grief weighing me down. I keep replaying conversations with Dad in my head. More like heated arguments over my future, until he gave up on me as a lost cause. That's what he called me, a lost cause.

Ironic that I can only prove I'm successful after he dies by selling his business and opening my dream restaurant. In the end, I'd finally reach my dream because of him. Just thinking about it makes me feel guilty. At the same time, what am I going to do with five car dealerships? He knew I had no experience and no interest. As far as I know, there's a manager at each location, but Dad was the final authority everything ran through. He had the vision, and he was the motor that kept everyone racing ahead, meeting and surpassing sales goals. From what I could tell, his employees feared him. Not the best motivator, but it sure worked. His way or the highway. No wonder he couldn't be flexible where I was concerned.

Our philosophies weren't so different in retrospect. I always say, bow to the master or do it yourself. His version was, bow to the master or get out. My gut does a slow roll. I don't want to be like his worst traits.

Paige pokes her head in the kitchen. "How's it going in here, maestro?"

"Maestro, huh?"

"You're conducting a symphony of flavors."

My assistants, Sara and Rick, titter. They're a married couple. Sara confessed she always thought Paige and I would get together. All of our fighting was rife with sexual tension. Of course, there was the irritated factor holding me back for a while. Paige hadn't yet acknowledged me as the boss.

"Hold up a minute." I step away from the stuffed chicken I was preparing and wash my hands. I need some Paige loving. She's not pregnant, so that takes the pressure off. I don't feel honor bound to propose. I'm glad. I'm still getting the hang of the relationship thing. Marriage comes with high expectations, and the last thing I want is to fail at it.

"Make it quick," she says. "I've got guests out here to entertain. Brooke has the day off."

"Then why're you checking on me?"

"Because you're cute."

This time Sara and Rick laugh out loud. I shoot them a dark look before taking Paige's hand and stepping outside with her to the deck. "I'm not cute. I'm handsome."

She rubs my jaw. "Mmm, I like the short beard, handsome."

"Do you think I'm too domineering?" I hate to ask, but thoughts of Dad have me worried. He wasn't great with people except for Mom, who's practically a saint.

"A bit, but not too much. You like to think you're the boss of everyone. It helps get things done in a chef situation, but you also recognize that I'm the boss in my domain."

I let out a breath. "Good. Cool."

"Where's this coming from?"

"Dad acted like the boss of everything and everyone. It's partly why we fought so much, but I'd like to think I'm not that bad. I don't want to continue that part of the legacy."

She rubs my arm. "You're not so bad."

I pull her into my arms, and she hugs me back, resting her cheek against my chest. Paige has been more of a comfort during this difficult time than I ever could've imagined.

I speak in a low voice near her ear. "I don't know what to do about my inheritance."

She pulls back to look at me. "It's yours. What do you want to do with it?"

"I want to sell it to someone who actually wants to run a car dealership, take the proceeds, and give half to Mom and use the other half to fund my dream. But Mom would be upset if I sold, and I don't want to hurt her."

"Maybe if you explain you'd have to give up your dream to take your dad's place, she'd sympathize with you."

"I tried that already. You saw how upset she got."

"I know, but emotions were running high right after the funeral. I think it would be worth another conversation."

I cross my arms and look out toward the tree line. "That takes out my bold declaration idea—here's how it's going to be. God, who does that sound like?" I turn back to her. "I'll try again."

"I support you no matter what you want to do."

I tip her chin up and kiss her. "I'm glad to hear that because I found the perfect place for my restaurant upstate."

"You did? I didn't know you were still looking." She pushes my shoulder. "I was supposed to do that. This is my field of expertise. Let me see the listing."

I pull my phone out and click over to it, where I left it saved. "It has an apple orchard, pear trees, and cherry trees."

"Mmm, pie." She scrolls down. "Where is this place? I don't know this county."

"It's a rural area about three hours away. I'd have to make it a destination, and do you know what could help with that?"

Her brows scrunch together as she reads the details on the listing. "What?"

"If you opened a bed and breakfast on the property. People could stay there and then go over to the restaurant conveniently located next door."

Her gaze snaps to mine. "You want me to go into business with you? Three hours away from my business?"

"Our businesses would be separate, but they'd complement each other. And we could be together."

She backs up a step. "I already have a bed and breakfast that I run. We're just getting things off the ground here. I'm the full-time innkeeper."

"So hire someone else to take your place here. What about Brooke?"

"She works part-time as an architect for residential clients.

She never wanted to be full-time here. Not to mention I don't have the funds to open another B&B."

"But I do. Well, I will." With Paige on board, I'm sure it would soften the blow for Mom over me selling the dealerships. She's wanted me to settle down for a long time. And I don't want to be three hours away from Paige. This way, everyone wins.

Paige's eyes widen. "You'd use your inheritance for me?"

"If it meant keeping you close, then yes."

She shakes her head. "I don't know. I mean, I appreciate the sentiment, but the inn means a lot to me. My sister and I came up with the concept and worked to build it together. And I'm close to family here."

"You could be close to me."

"You mean marriage?"

I hesitate. "Maybe. Down the road."

She bites her lower lip. "I'm sorry, I can't give up so much for a maybe."

"What do you want, a proposal?" I slap my thigh, gearing up for it. "Right now? Fine. Marry me."

"That is *not* a proposal. That's a demand."

"It's an order. You can't have it both ways. I'm stepping up."

Her eyes well, and my chest tightens in sympathy. "You don't just propose to someone because you think that's what they want. I don't want it this way. You're only saying it to convince me to move with you." She looks away. "I'm going for a walk with Bear."

She rushes into the inn.

I chase after her.

"Don't follow me!" she says, hurrying toward her apartment.

I catch up to her before she reaches the stairs, grabbing her from behind.

She struggles for a moment, and I hang on, pinning her arms to her sides. "Hold on. Hear me out."

She gives up and sighs. "You don't even know for sure you're selling the car dealerships."

I loosen my hold but don't let go. "I'd sell in a heartbeat if it meant we could stay together."

She shifts in my arms. "Why don't you open a restaurant here? We could add on to the inn for your restaurant, or knock down the old garage and put a new structure there. Maybe even check in with my neighbor about selling his house. He's an elderly widower. Make him a good offer, and he might be happy to let it go. Then you could have a house to convert to a restaurant and some land for a huge garden. We both get what we want."

"Not quite. I want a working farm. I can't do that in the space there. I know the place you're talking about, and it's not right for my purposes."

"I'm sure you could make do. Plus there's a few farmers' markets nearby, and the fish market isn't far."

"That isn't my dream. This place I found gives me everything I want."

She exhales sharply. "I'm sorry, but I'm not following you there. I want to keep my business just like it is and run it with Brooke. I want to be near Wyatt and Kayla. I'm going to be an aunt soon, and I want to be able to pop in and visit my niece or nephew whenever I can. And I'm sure it won't be long before Kayla's pregnant too." Her voice cracks.

I study her expression. Her eyes reflect longing. She wants that life for herself.

"You want to be like them," I say. "Pregnant. Caring for a baby."

"Yes," she says softly.

I take a deep breath. "I'll give you that too if you come with me."

"This isn't a negotiation." She pushes away. "I guess this is goodbye."

"What do you mean it's goodbye?" I bark.

Her jaw sets. "Because we want different things."

"I said I would get you pregnant. I'm giving you everything you want."

"But it's not because you want it. You want everything your way—your place upstate done your way with me as an add-on. I get that you need to live your life your way, but it's not my way."

The hair on the nape of my neck stands up, my breath coming faster. *Everything your way.* No. I'm not like him. It's not my way or nothing. I'm offering something big to her—a future with everything we both want.

"Paige, I'm not bossing about this. I'm giving."

She shakes her head. "You're giving to get. There's a difference."

I throw my hands up. "You're impossible! I quit! Find another chef."

"Fine!"

She rushes upstairs to her apartment. This time I let her.

I'm offering everything she could possibly want. She's so stubborn and hardheaded. Too damn independent.

I turn on my heel and stride back to the kitchen to finish my job for the very last time. Fuck it. I don't need the aggravation.

## 15

*Paige*

I miss Spencer. He hasn't called or texted in a week. It's Monday, so I know he's off work today. Maybe I'll just pop by his place to see how he's doing. Maybe he was just out of sorts over his dad's death earlier, and he didn't mean it the way things came out. But is it so much to want a romantic proposal that doesn't sound like it's a means to an end?

I wasn't saying marry me or forget it. I just think if two people are going to get married, it shouldn't come as a surprise. It should be something they talk about for a while, looking to the future. We've only been dating for two months. That's too soon for a spontaneous proposal. Though he did say he'd marry me when there was a chance I could be pregnant. In some ways, he's a traditional man with a sense of honor and duty. That's a good thing.

Okay, I'm not giving up on Spencer.

I show up at his rented house by the lake, but he's not home. I brought Bear with me, hoping his cute puppy face would cheer Spencer up. Everyone feels happier with Bear around.

Maybe Spencer went to visit his mom, or he could be at a lawyer's office, figuring out how to sell his dad's business. I sit on the front porch steps of his place to think, letting Bear sniff around the porch. In hindsight, I shouldn't have been so hasty in my goodbye to Spencer. I guess I got scared to hear him spouting all these things I would normally love to hear when they felt so wrong.

His truck pulls into the driveway, and my heart pounds. I should've prepared a speech or something.

He steps out, dressed casually in a white T-shirt and faded jeans. "What're you doing here?"

"I wanted to see if you were okay."

He runs a hand through his hair, blows out a breath, and slams the door of his truck. "No, I'm not okay."

I cross to him, guiding Bear with me. Spencer takes one look at Bear, and his whole demeanor softens. He turns to me, hurt in his eyes.

I give him a hug. He allows it but doesn't return it. I swallow hard and pull away. "I feel like things got a little heated last time we talked. I should've cut you some slack since you're still grieving."

"Don't worry about it." He strides past me and walks to the front door, unlocking it.

"Wait. What's going on with you? Did you buy that place upstate?"

"Have to sell my inheritance first. I'm heading to Mom's place to let her know before I meet with the lawyer."

"You think she'll be okay with it?"

He exhales sharply and turns to face me. "No. It would've been a helluva lot better if you were on board. She might forgive me if she thought I was settling down. I'm a disappointment to both my parents. That's just something I have to live with."

He lets himself into his house.

I scoop up Bear and hurry into his place, uninvited. The living room is neat as usual. A blue sofa with neatly placed throw pillows, a glass coffee table and glass end tables without a spot on them. He cares for his things down to the last detail. That bodes well for running his own business. He'll care and take the time to do it right.

"What if I went with you to see your mom for moral support?" I ask.

He looks to the ceiling and levels a hard look at me. "Why would you want to do that? She's either going to scream or cry. Neither of which will make for a fun visit. Besides, you broke up with me."

"I'm unbreaking us up."

He groans. "You drive me insane, woman. You say we want different things, and when I offer to give you everything you want, you dump me."

I take a moment, drawing on my last bit of patience. He's still not getting why I was upset by his negotiation-style proposal. Spencer's going through a difficult time and can't help it if he sounds like a wounded bear. He *is* a wounded bear. Oh, Bear!

"I'll bring Bear with us for a visit," I say, holding him up. "He'll lighten the mood and make your mom feel better."

"She's more of a cat person. She used to have a cat, but he died."

I hold Bear close, pressing my cheek to his cheek as we look at Spencer. "Come on, look at this face. Who wouldn't love a little puppy face like this?"

He tries to glare at me and Bear cheek-to-cheek, but he can't resist the irresistible puppy face. He gives Bear a stroke over his little golden head. "That might work."

Hope spears through me. Does that mean we're back together? I'm afraid to ask.

I keep an upbeat tone. "Great, let's go. Should you let your mom know you're bringing us along?"

"Nah. Let's surprise her with Bear. I have to take care of a few things here first."

"Oh, well, should I meet you later?"

"Might as well come with me. I'm going to your brother's house."

My eyes widen. "Why?"

"Because Sydney owns The Horseman Inn. I want to see if she can gradually reduce my hours as I work on building my own restaurant. I don't want to cut ties completely."

"Why not? If you sell your dad's business, you'll have plenty of money."

"It's not about the money. It's about artistic integrity. I don't want them to rush my replacement. I built that place's reputation. I'm not throwing that away."

"It has been around for four generations."

He narrows his eyes.

I hold up a palm. "But you brought it into its culinary glory."

"Thank you," he says curtly. "The old chef served up tired recipes with frozen ingredients. Do you know he added French fries or a baked potato to every dish? No imagination."

"You're the *artiste*."

"Now you're yanking my chain."

I bite back a smile. "Was it my French accent?"

"It's true, so I'll let it slide."

"Are we good?" I hold my breath, telling myself I need to be okay with whatever he says next.

He runs a hand over his face. "I don't know what to do about you, and that's a first for me. I'm usually quick to cut ties, but I don't want to end it."

Relief floods me, making my limbs light. "That's good."

"But you're right that we want different things. You're invested in Summerdale and your business here. My dream is somewhere else. What're we going to do, commute?"

"Three hours is a long commute." I put my hand on his arm. "Look, this is a difficult emotional time for you. Don't make any big decisions right now about me or anything else."

"I need to move quickly before I lose the property."

"Well, you won't lose me if you take your time figuring out where I fit in your life. Later, down the line."

He searches my expression. "I don't see how anything changes down the line, but I appreciate your support. You and Bear will make a nice buffer with my mom and your brother."

"Is Wyatt being too…" *Overprotective, overbearing.* "Wyatt?"

"He'll let up on me if he sees us together. Let's go."

I follow him to his truck. "What do you mean? Did he say something to you?"

He unlocks it and climbs in. I settle Bear in the seat behind us and take my seat.

Spencer gives me a deadpan look. "Wyatt told me to get my head out of my ass and make up with you. He said you were more irritable than usual and the usual was bad enough."

I shrug one shoulder. "That sounds like him."

He pulls out of the driveway and turns onto the street. He doesn't say anything until we get to my brother's house. I'm quiet, trying to be a silent support instead of another cause of aggravation in his life. I love this man, and I need to remember he's going through something right now.

He parks and turns off the truck, staring straight ahead.

"Are you okay?"

He turns to me, his voice gruff with emotion. "I missed you."

I throw my arms around him. "I missed you too."

He kisses me. "Please don't fight with me. I can't take it right now."

I give him my best attempt at a sweet smile. "I'll be sweet as pie."

"Right. That's not the Paige I know and love."

I shove his shoulder. "Hey!"

"Better," he says, resting his forehead against mine. "Much better."

∼

*Spencer*

"So you made up," Wyatt says over the noise of his dogs, Snowball and Rexie, barking their heads off at us at the front door. Probably doesn't help that Bear is matching their excitement. Wyatt's around my height, six feet, with wavy brown hair and the same whisky eyes as Paige. He studies his sister's expression and must seem satisfied because he lets us into the house.

He orders his dogs to stand down, and they stop the ruckus and circle me, sniffing curiously. Snowball is a white shih tzu, and Rexie is a tan pit bull mix. Bear races through the house, probably looking for the other dogs' chew toys.

Wyatt gestures between us. "Good for you. Now I can finally get a break from nonstop bitching."

"Hey, I wasn't bitching about him," Paige protests. "Don't make it sound like that."

Wyatt shoots me a wry look, then turns to her. "No, it was more of a generalized bitching about the world when we all knew the real problem."

His wife, Sydney, appears in the front hall. Her long auburn hair is down from its usual ponytail. A small baby bump shows through her blue V-neck T-shirt. "Would you please let them all the way in? Spencer says he needs to discuss something important." She smiles at Paige. "Hello, Auntie Paige. We had the ultrasound. Come see the picture on the refrigerator."

"Oh, yeah? Did you find out the sex?" Paige asks, following her to the kitchen.

I join the group in the kitchen gathered around a stainless steel refrigerator. Four red dot magnets on the corners of the ultrasound picture hold it in place on the door.

Paige peers closely at the image. "I think it's a girl."

Sydney elbows her. "You can't tell that. The technician made sure the image was taken when the baby was shifted slightly away."

"Pretty sure I know what the boy part looks like," Paige says.

I squint my eyes and lean closer, but all I see is a black-and-white fuzzy picture. I see the head and the curve of body, one tiny hand. Can't tell if it has the requisite part.

"We want to be surprised," Sydney says through her teeth. "I was the only girl in my family, and Wyatt was the only boy in his. We're happy either way, right, babe?"

Wyatt pulls her to him and puts his hand on her baby bump. "It has to be a boy. We can't agree on a girl name."

"That's because you want to name her Trouble or Pandora," Sydney returns.

I laugh out loud. Paige shakes her head at her brother.

"See?" Sydney points at me. "People will laugh at her."

Wyatt stands his ground. "No one will mess with a girl named Trouble. They'll steer far away. And there's nothing wrong with Pandora, it's a goddess's name."

Sydney jabs him in the chest. "No one will go near Pandora if they know their Greek mythology. Also trouble. Are you trying to scare guys away from our daughter already?"

"Think of it as a protective force field," he says. "She won't need my interference when the name says it all."

Sydney shoots him a deadpan look.

"What's the boy name?" I ask.

"Andrew Matthew Winters," Wyatt says proudly.

"Andrew is after my dad," Sydney says.

"And Matthew is after ours," Paige says. She gives Wyatt's arm a squeeze. "That's real nice to carry on the grandfathers' names like that. It's like they get to live on after death in the next generation."

"Unless it's a girl," I say. "Then here comes trouble."

Wyatt laughs and claps me on the shoulder.

"Anyway," Sydney says, dragging out the word. "Let's have a seat at the kitchen table. Anyone want a drink?"

"I'll get it," Wyatt says instantly. "Go ahead and take a seat."

"It's no problem," Sydney says. "The doctor says it's good for me to be active."

Wyatt puts his hand on the small of her back and guides her to the kitchen table in an open dining area next to the kitchen. "You're on your feet enough at work. Let's not push it."

Paige leans close to me and whispers, "Overbearing brother in action."

"He's taking care of her," I whisper back.

We hang back, watching Wyatt pull out Sydney's chair and get her situated at the table. Nothing wrong with that. Any decent man would do the same. My dad...I swallow over the lump of emotion lodged in my throat. Dad took care of Mom in a loving way. He took care of me too, until I stepped away from the path he'd set and we started arguing constantly. He set a fine example of what a good man is like for the most part. I have those values of honor and integrity. He taught me to treat women with respect. Mom did too, I suppose, just by being such a loving influence on me. I turn away, the stinging in my eyes threatening to turn into tears.

Wyatt passes me on his way to the kitchen. "What can I get...oh, hey, are you okay?"

Paige's head whips toward mine. "Do you need a minute?"

"Just point me toward the restroom," I say. "This way, right?" I walk down the hallway toward the living room. I was here before for a charity calendar photo shoot.

"It's the first door on your left," Paige calls.

I hear Wyatt's concerned voice behind me, talking to Paige. Everyone knows I lost Dad recently. I took a day off work for the funeral.

I splash some cold water on my face in the bathroom and take a few deep breaths. If I fall apart now, I'm never going to get through this conversation, and I definitely won't be in any shape to face Mom and tell her my plans.

I return to the kitchen table a few minutes later. Everyone has glasses of water, and there's one left for me next to Paige's chair. I sit down and take a long drink.

"How're you doing?" Sydney asks gently.

"We know it's hard," Wyatt says. "We both lost our dads too."

I nod once and clear my throat. "Thank you. So I'll just get to the point. I inherited Dad's business, and I plan to sell it and use the proceeds to open my own restaurant. I have my eye on a property upstate. It'll take time to build it, so I wanted to let you know now to give you some time to find my replacement."

"Oh, wow, Spencer, this is big news," Sydney says. "Your cooking has been such a huge draw for the restaurant. I don't know if we could ever find your equal."

I give Paige a sideways glance that's just shy of gloating. She gives me a small close-lipped smile.

"I've really enjoyed working there and with both of you," I say.

"We hate to lose you, but I understand wanting to go out on your own," Wyatt says. "I'd love your help in reviewing the candidates, and by that I mean actually tasting their cooking."

"Absolutely," I say.

They both stare at me, seeming lost in thought. I surprised them. I've been working there for more than a year, and they always rave about how much business I'm bringing in for them. Still, my own restaurant was always the dream.

"What kind of business are you selling?" Wyatt finally asks.

"No," Sydney says.

"I'm just asking," Wyatt says.

"Dad owned a successful chain of car dealerships," I say. "Used and new cars."

"How many and where?" Wyatt asks.

"Five. All in New York, but farther north. Closest one is an hour from here."

Wyatt gets a gleam in his eyes and leans in. "I might know a couple of guys who'd be interested in buying the business and hiring someone else to run it. I might even know someone who'd want to buy it and run it themselves."

Sydney waves her hand in the air. "Hello! Your pregnant wife here. With our business and the baby coming, this is *not* the time to take on more responsibility. An hour or more is a long commute and a big time commitment."

Wyatt gives her a smile that verges on a smirk. "I'm happy to be needed, but I wasn't going to run it by myself. I'd look over the books and think of it as an investment. Someone else would do the day-to-day."

Sydney shakes her head. "You couldn't help getting involved. I know you."

"She's right," Paige puts in.

"No one asked you," Wyatt says, reaching over and giving Paige's hair a tug.

She rolls her eyes.

Wyatt turns to me. "Send me the details. I'll put out some feelers for you in the meantime."

"Thanks, I appreciate the help. I've never sold a business before." I stand. "I'd better get going. I just wanted to tell you face-to-face about the job situation. Now I have to break the news to Mom that I want to sell. She thinks I should take over the business as Dad wanted."

Paige joins me, putting her hand on my arm in a show of support. I'm so glad she's by my side again.

"Oh, it was a gift with strings," Sydney says. "That's rough. You take as much time as you need to get your stuff together. You didn't take much time off to grieve."

"I'm fine," I say. "I prefer to be working."

Sydney hugs me and then Paige and excuses herself to the bathroom. Paige scoops up Bear from the large kitchen, where he was scouting for crumbs. She cuddles him close like he's a baby. Soon he'll be too big for that.

Wyatt walks us to the door, and his dogs follow him. "Did your dad happen to sell any classic cars?"

"No, just the regular kind. Mostly Nissans, Jeeps, and Chevys."

"I picked up a 1963 Corvette Stingray split-window coupe to tinker with in the garage, but I wouldn't mind owning a dealership with first dibs on every classic car that comes in."

Snowball sniffs at my shoe, and Rexie circles around to sniff my butt. I shoo Rexie away.

"You're *not* buying a dealership," Paige says to Wyatt. "Listen to your wife. You need to work on building your dynasty here."

Wyatt grins. "Sydney's been talking about our dynasty ever since she got pregnant. God, I love that woman." He claps a hand on my shoulder. "Good luck with the mom talk. Keep me in the loop on the dealerships."

"Thanks, I will."

Paige kisses his scruffy cheek. "You're a dad now. Go do your thing."

He smiles widely. "I'm secretly hoping for a girl. I did help raise three younger sisters, so I know what to do."

"You're only two years older than me," Paige says.

Wyatt goes on like she hasn't spoken. "Trouble Winters. Look out, world! Here comes Trouble!"

She shoves his shoulder. "You just want to say 'here comes Trouble' every time she walks in the room."

He chuckles, heading back to his wife. His dogs trot after him.

Paige and I head back to my truck. It's a load off my mind with Wyatt in my corner. He's a savvy businessman who's already run successful businesses and sold them. "Your brother's a good guy."

Paige smiles. "He is. Overbearing, but he has a good heart."

As soon as we're both in the truck, Bear tucked in back, she says, "It's okay to let Wyatt help, but don't sell to him because he'll take over. He can't help himself. And, as you heard, Sydney won't be happy to have him so far away."

"But it would be such an easy quick sale."

"There's nothing easy about Wyatt and business. You'll be dealing with his demands, and it could get messy since you're involved with me."

*Is she thinking in the future we'll be married? I thought she shot down that idea.*

"Because I'd have to see him at family events?" I ask.

She blinks a few times, like she's thinking up a good response. "Better not to mix business with your girlfriend's family. That's all."

I cup her jaw and kiss her. She's coming around to the idea of a future with me. "I'll take your word for it."

## 16

That talk went better than I thought. Let's hope the next one goes as well. The drive gives me a little time to think about how to explain to Mom in the most rational calm way that me selling the business isn't betraying Dad. It's passing it on to more experienced hands, where it will probably keep going successfully, while also letting me pursue my dream. She could pursue her dreams too with her half of the proceeds. I'm not even sure if she has dreams. She was always just so dedicated to our family. I need to spend more time getting to know Mom. It's just us now.

Paige pipes up, "If your mom's not cool with Bear, I'll just hang out on the back deck with him while you have your talk."

"You're supposed to be there as moral support. Your words."

"Well, I don't want to upset her."

"She's going to be upset no matter what," I say grimly.

She pats my shoulder. "Let's keep positive. Maybe she'll understand and support your dream. I do."

"Even if that takes me away from you."

"We can meet halfway. An hour and a half commute for both of us is doable, right?"

"I still think you should come with me."

"My business is just getting off the ground."

I let out a breath. One thing at a time. First I need to be sure I can get the funds to buy the property I want. It's not like Mom could stop me legally. It's just that I don't want our relationship to sour over it. Everything has to be done with great care for her feelings.

Paige fills me in on all the latest at the animal shelter's Best Friends Care program. She's excited she got to meet the famous actress Harper Ellis, who established the program there. Paige is so into their mission she's even thinking about fostering another dog after Bear goes to live with his new owner. It takes a big heart to love a dog and then let them go to another person after a year. I'm not sure if Paige realizes how hard that will be, or maybe she does, and that's why she wants to take on another dog.

"I'll contribute to the program too," I say. "It sounds awesome."

"Great! Wyatt and Harper already donated enough to fund them for the year, but I'm sure they could save some for next year."

"Did Wyatt help you pay for the inn?"

"No way. I told you he takes over when he's involved with a business. Brooke and I were very careful not to let him even see the inn until the renovation was complete. He means well, and I appreciate that, but, you know, boundaries. Gotta have them."

"I guess. Just seems like it would've been easier on you."

"We made the right choice. Trust me. Now tell me about your plans for your restaurant."

I smile just thinking about it. "The front reception area will be rustic, done with wood and wrought iron, and there'll be a large open dining room with floor-to-ceiling windows to take in the view. Skylights for more natural light. I want it to feel like the outside and inside merge together. The tables will be a glossy dark wood with cushioned chairs to encourage people to linger over their meal. At night, sconces on the walls and small candle votives on the tables will make a soft glow. Everything set for a relaxing experience."

"That sounds lovely," she says. "Bar?"

"Yeah, a separate room for a bar for when people are waiting, or if they just want a quick bite. I don't want noise to carry from the bar to the dining area."

"How many do you hope to host?"

"Fifty. I don't want it to be too huge, but you need a big enough dining room to keep the place profitable."

"It's too bad this property you've got your eye on is so far away because I worked with a great interior designer, Skylar, on the inn. She's still building her portfolio, so she's more affordable. You'd like working with her to achieve your vision."

She tells me all about Skylar and also the contractor for the inn, Gage, whom she also thinks highly of. I'm glad she had such a positive experience. As for me, I'm on my own. That's okay. I'll find the right people.

A while later, familiar landmarks come into view, and I get tenser. I grip the steering wheel tighter, rehearsing my speech. *Mom, I'm grateful for the inheritance. And I hope you understand that this is nothing against Dad, but I'd like to use it for my dream restaurant.* Simple and to the point.

I pull into the driveway of the house I grew up in, a large Tudor-style home. It suddenly occurs to me that Mom might want to sell it. My gut tenses at the thought. It's a lot of house for one person living alone. It would be hard to know I didn't have my childhood home to come back to. Although, if she does say she wants to sell before I tell her I want to sell the business, maybe it'll put us on more equal footing. Both of us moving on to something that works for us.

I blow out a breath, not ready to face her yet.

"You got this." Paige kisses my cheek and gets out to retrieve Bear from the back seat.

I get out of the truck and wait for Paige. I'm glad for the buffer, though I'm not sure anything will soften the blow for Mom.

I ring the bell.

Mom answers a few moments later. She looks better than the last time I saw her, a little more color in her cheeks and no bags under her eyes. She's wearing a short-sleeved yellow sweater and white pants. "Oh, I didn't know you were bringing Paige. Nice to see you. Uh-oh, your dog." She gestures toward Bear. "Cute as he is, I'm not sure how he'll take to Stella and Charlie. Those are my new kittens."

*Mom got kittens?*

"It's good for Bear to socialize," Paige says. "I'm supposed to introduce him to lots of people and different environments. He's very gentle and social. But if you like, I could put him in the backyard."

Mom steps back, gesturing us in with a smile. "Come on in. Let's see how he is with cats."

I'm so relieved to see her smiling I find myself smiling.

Paige leads Bear inside. "He's never met a cat. Are they friendly?"

I follow, looking around for the cats.

"They're just as friendly as can be," Mom says. "Brother and sister kittens. They're napping together on the sofa." She looks behind her to the sofa, which is empty. "Oh, they must've gotten scared. I'll be right back."

Paige sits on the sofa and orders Bear to sit on the floor next to her, praising him lavishly for obeying. His tongue lolls out of the side of his mouth in doggy glory. "Guess we didn't need Bear to cheer her up."

I sit next to Paige. "Guess not." It's been two weeks since Dad died, and it seems Mom's doing okay. She's grieving like me, but she's not withdrawing from the world. She found something to bring her comfort.

Mom returns from the kitchen, cradling two black and white kittens in her arms. They're mostly black with white on their chests, paws, and noses. Mom sits on Paige's other side, and Bear leaps up, barking at the kittens, who arch in alarm, their tails puffing out. Paige hushes Bear while Mom keeps the kittens calm, cooing to them. A moment later, dog and cats are sniffing each other.

Mom puts the kittens on the floor, and they wander

around Bear, sniffing at him. One of them bats his tail, and he whirls in a circle to stop it. Mom's smiling, watching their antics.

"It's great that you got kittens," I say. "They brighten things up."

Mom turns serious. "How're you doing?"

I let out a breath. "Sad, you know, but also making plans for the future."

"Is that what you wanted to talk to me about? Dad's business?"

"Yes." I try to come up with the rehearsed words, but looking at her expectant expression, her gentle eyes, my mind goes blank.

Paige shifts to sit on the floor near Bear, leaning back against Dad's recliner. "Spencer's a fantastic chef. Have you stopped by The Horseman Inn to try his cooking?"

"He's made Thanksgiving and Christmas dinner for us every year since he was in high school, but we never went to one of his restaurants."

"Because of Dad," I say. It's not a question.

Mom watches her cats as they jump on Bear's constantly moving tail, being playful. He's good with them, not growling or snapping, just shifting away. "We knew you were good at what you do. Who else would serve us a five-course gourmet meal?"

"I'd like to do that again in my own restaurant," I say. "Dad's made it possible for me to follow my dream."

Mom sighs. "You mean sell his business to strangers."

"Paige's brother knows a lot of people in the business world. He could vet them and make sure we get someone good in place. The dealerships will live on, just not under my leadership."

She shakes her head. "He couldn't let go of his dream of sharing it with you." She scoots closer, takes my hand, and gives it a squeeze. "I told him to let it go and find someone else he could train to eventually take over the business, but once he got something in his head, he never veered from his path. I suppose that's what made him so good at what he did. He set sales goals and met them. Every time."

"I know."

She gives me a shaky smile. "Without Dad here, I'm a little lost. He was always the one with the plan, you know?"

I nod.

"I need to start making decisions on my own for my future, and you have to do the same."

"It's just you seemed so upset when I mentioned selling the business before."

"I've been talking to a grief counselor. Every day, actually, and she's helped a lot. Nothing will ever be the same. Not for me or you. One step at a time I'll find my way to a different way of life." She wipes at a tear. "Besides, I don't really want to go back to the dealerships without him there. He was such a big presence."

I give her a hug, my throat tight. This is hard.

She sniffles, straightening and wiping a tear away. "I always wished you could've had a brother or sister, but it just wasn't possible. It would've been good for you, and you wouldn't have had so much pressure on you to take over for Dad." She puts her hand on my cheek. "My boy. I'm so proud of you."

My eyes sting. "Thanks," I manage over the lump in my throat.

She nods. "Your dad was proud of you too. He always bragged about your holiday dinners at work. And he enjoyed the leftovers with a look of wonder on his face. He just couldn't bring himself to admit it. I think he believed if he encouraged you too much as a chef, you'd never come on board with him."

*So misguided.*

I sniffle, my eyes stinging. "I knew he liked the food. It was the only time he stopped talking, and he always cleared his plate." My voice chokes.

Paige hands us both tissues, her own eyes shiny with tears.

"Thanks, sweetheart," Mom says.

"No problem," Paige says.

"Paige, why don't you have a seat next to Spencer?" Mom gets up and goes to her chair.

Paige sits next to me and tucks her hand in mine. I can hardly believe how smoothly that went down. I feared Mom would disown me. Then again, I'm her only child. She's kinda stuck with me.

We're quiet for a moment. Bear sighs. We all look over. Bear's lying down, worn out by the kittens, who're curled up against his belly.

"Aww," Paige whispers. "He's even good with kittens."

"They wore him out," I say.

Mom smiles, looking at Bear with the cats. "You know, Dad and I planned on retiring to the Florida Keys down the line."

My heart kicks harder. It's the very thing I expected yet wasn't quite ready to hear. My family home gone, the memories tied up here closed off forever. "Yeah? Are you thinking of moving?"

"Not now. I need time to, you know, grieve, but maybe in a year. Would you visit me there?"

"Mom, of course! I'd visit you anywhere. You're stuck with me for life."

Paige sniffles. "These tears are contagious."

I kiss Paige's temple and go over to crouch next to Mom's chair. "Anything you need, I'll take care of it."

She gives my shoulder a squeeze. "You have all your dad's best qualities."

"And yours. I wouldn't be the man I am today without you. I love you, Mom."

Tears flow down her cheeks. "I love you too."

I give her a hug, and a cold nose hits my neck. Bear wants in on this. As soon as I pull away, the kittens leap onto Mom's lap.

I back up as Mom gets cuddles from Bear, Stella, and Charlie. The animals know when someone needs that extra loving. And then I turn to Paige, see the love in her eyes, and know I have to find a way for us to work together.

I sit next to her on the sofa and wrap an arm around her shoulders. "You're stuck with me too."

She leans against my shoulder. "Lucky me."

I pull back. "Was that sarcasm from my future wife?"

She nods, her cheeks flushing as she whispers, "I can't believe you said that in front of your mom."

"Future wife?" Mom asks. "Is there something you'd like to tell me?"

"Mom, I love her. I just told her we're getting married."

She turns to Paige. "And is this okay with you?"

Paige smiles, her eyes welling. "I love him with all my heart. He's stuck with me too."

Mom's lips purse. "It wasn't a very romantic proposal, Spencer."

"Oh, I haven't agreed," Paige says. "The romantic proposal will happen when the time's right. I won't be engaged spontaneously or under orders. There's a time and place for this kind of thing."

I kiss her cheek. "But you acknowledge it's happening."

"Yes."

Pure joy bursts through my chest. I didn't think I could feel such joy, especially so soon after loss. I grab her and pull her into my lap, stroking her cheek. "I'll take good care of you and any kids we have down the line. Pets, everyone. You can count on me."

She giggles. "Even the pets?"

"You're all under my domain."

"How about we share that domain?"

"Deal."

"I'm finally going to have grandkids to spoil!" Mom exclaims, rushing over to hug Paige.

I stand and join in for a family hug, glancing over at Dad's recliner. I'd like to think he's smiling down at us. After all, I made the love of his life happy and gave her something to look forward to—grandchildren. One day in the not-too-distant future. Dad will still be a part of things. I'm his true legacy, not the business, passing on the best parts of him to my kids one day. Honor and integrity above all.

And with that, the guilt lifts.

I kiss Paige's hair. The woman who battled me, loved me, and supported me. She gave me everything, and I'll spend the rest of my life giving back to her.

# EPILOGUE

**Two weeks later...**

*Paige*

*Pop!* Champagne time!

"Here's to living your dream!" I clink my glass against Spencer's. We're at my place, celebrating the successful sale of his inheritance. Wyatt's connections made for a fast sale to a business associate who loves cars. My happiness for Spencer is only a little dimmed by my worry over him moving three hours away to his dream property. But I support him no matter what. I want him to be happy.

We both sip our champagne. He sets his glass on the coffee table and turns to me. My heart kicks up speed at the news I've been dreading—he's leaving Summerdale. And me.

He takes a deep breath. "So, I've given this a lot of thought—"

Bear leaps on the sofa between us.

"Down," I tell him and then praise him lavishly for jumping back to the floor. He sits facing me, his dark eyes looking expectantly at me. I rub him behind the ears, and his eyes go half-mast in doggy bliss. Soon Bear will be big, and I don't want his new owner to have to fight him for space on the sofa.

Spencer's suddenly close, kissing along my neck and lowering me under him on the sofa. Oh, this is much better than a heavy relationship talk. I can feel Bear's eyes on us and hope he gets bored soon and falls asleep.

Spencer brushes my hair back from my face and cups my jaw. "This is the part where we talk about the relationship."

I swallow hard. "Okay. I should say up front that I just want you to be happy."

One corner of his mouth lifts. "I'm glad you feel that way because I think we should merge our dreams."

*Is this a proposal? Does he want me to move three hours away to his dream property?* "What do you mean by merge?"

He strokes a sensitive spot just under my ear with his thumb. "I mean, we should live and work together." He kisses me, settling between my legs. All thoughts fly from my mind as a rush of pleasure floods my senses. His heat, his taste, the delicious pressure in just the right spot.

He lifts his head and turns to Bear, who's watching us. "Go get your ball."

Bear dashes off to the cardboard box of toys I keep for him in the corner.

"You know he's a retriever," I say. "He's coming right back with that."

Spencer nips my bottom lip. "So here's what I'm thinking—"

"I like the way you didn't just issue a statement of fact." *Also known as an order.* He's prone to those, being the boss of his kitchen. I stroke the hair at the nape of his neck. "Now it sounds like I get a say too."

"Of course you do. You agreed to be my wife."

I smile. "That's not official, but, yes, at some point when the time is right, I'd like that."

He kisses me long and deep. When he finally lets me up for air, he says, "I made an offer to your neighbor, the widower, to buy his house. He's considering it. If you're willing to do the whole thing in a private sale, owner to owner, it could sweeten the deal."

I blink, truly surprised. He hadn't said a word about it. "Okay," I say slowly.

He flashes a smile. "That house is for us. The B&B and restaurant would be together right here on your property. I'm hoping we can use part of his land to expand the garden. Maybe plant some apple trees and keep some chickens over there."

A burst of adrenaline shoots through my limbs. I'm both elated and concerned. It sounds great for us, but it isn't his dream. I push at his chest, and he sits up. "What about your dream property upstate with the orchard, garden, and all the animals?"

Bear barks. His ball is at Spencer's feet.

"Go get your firehose," Spencer orders.

Bear cocks his head.

"Firehose."

Bear runs back to his toy box.

I exhale sharply. "Can you please stop playing with my dog long enough to discuss our future?"

Spencer stands and scoops me up right off the sofa. I don't even squeak. I'm getting used to his sudden moves of affection. "Bedroom time. No dogs allowed."

I rub his chest. "What about your dream property? You can't do everything you wanted here."

"I realized part of the reason I wanted a huge place upstate was to prove to my parents that I'm a success. Maybe they'd even stop by for once to see me in action. Things are different now, and well, I don't have anything to prove to anyone. I'm about to achieve exactly what I wanted, my own restaurant."

I press my lips together, trying not to smile despite the happiness bubbling up. "Are you sure?"

"You've got a garden. We've got Bear—"

"Only until he's a year old."

Bear runs over and drops his firehose toy at Spencer's feet. Spencer and I exchange an impressed look.

"Good job," Spencer says. "Go get the rope toy. Rope."

Bear dashes off.

Spencer walks over the threshold of my bedroom and shuts the door behind us. "Now where were we?"

"You were saying you'd give up your dream and settle for just a garden and a foster dog, but—"

He kisses me, silencing my worry. "I'm not settling. You're my dream. The two of us together is all I want."

I beam, feeling light and weightless. I could float away on a cloud of happiness if he weren't carrying me. Ha!

I stroke his short beard. "What about the fresh milk and butter from your cow?"

He tosses me on the bed and pounces on me. "Woman, haven't you been listening? All I want is you."

I wrap my arms around him. "That's all?"

"And a restaurant. If you're willing to merge with me, that would be the perfect—"

I cut him off with a passionate kiss. "I'm ready to merge with you." I lower my voice to a sexy purr. "In *every* way."

He pulls my shirt off with a low hum of approval. "I like the sound of that."

We strip in record time and collide in a rush, suddenly ravenous for each other.

"I love you," he says hoarsely. *Kiss. Longer kiss.*

"I love you too."

And then there are no words. Only a fiery rush of lust and love as we merge, body and soul, sealing a promise of our new future together.

Here it is, the big moment. My former nemesis and now beloved Spencer stands next to me in front of the detached two-car garage on the large side lot of the inn. This will be the future spot of Spencer's, his new restaurant. We have plenty of land, and the town council agreed it was a good addition to the inn's property. The neighbors were okay with it too. Everyone in town is a fan of Spencer's cooking.

After this construction is complete, we plan to renovate the neighboring house we now own. We got it! With an above-market offer and a private sale, it was a quick deal. My sister Brooke, the brilliant architect, is coming up with a cool plan for the renovation. Of course, I had to email the editor at *Leisure Travel* with an update on the restaurant joining our inn, and they're on board to do a piece on us next summer. *Score!*

I'm still waiting on the next wedding at the inn to pitch to *Bride Special*. I'm hoping it's mine. No, we're not officially engaged. No ring. No romantic proposal. Yet.

"You sure about this?" Spencer asks me. "No turning back. You're never gonna get rid of me after this. I'll be right in your yard."

I grin. "This time if we fight, I know a sexy way we can make up."

He cups my jaw and kisses me.

Someone clears their throat.

I turn to face Gage, the contractor we used for the inn, who's going to work on the new restaurant for us. He's in his twenties, a big muscled guy with short brown hair that's shaved on the sides. Brooke says he's a *get the hell out of my way so I can do my job* kind of guy, and she's right. I like that about him. We've also got Skylar here, the interior designer we used for the inn. She's kinda family now since her brother Max married my sister Brooke. I brought her here today to go over the early stages of design.

Gage stares at me, his expression stone. Spencer and I are holding up the garage demolition.

"Can you get a before picture of us in front of it?" I ask, holding out my phone to Gage.

He grunts and takes the phone. He's not much of a talker.

Skylar, a pretty brunette with long hair and a perpetually sunny demeanor, gestures toward us. "Make sure you get the inn in the background."

"I got it," Gage grumbles, backing up and angling so he can get the inn in the picture too.

Spencer puts his arm around my shoulders. "Say Bear."

"Oh, Bear! Let me get him out here too."

Gage lets out a manly sigh. "You know my guys are on the clock, right?"

His crew is hanging out on the front lawn with assorted tools.

"Yes, yes. I just need to commemorate the event properly."

I dash inside the inn and upstairs to my apartment, where Bear is sleeping in his crate on a soft bed. "Wake up, picture time." I open the crate and pull out my fur baby, cuddling him close. "This is going everywhere—the inn's photo album, the website, all of our marketing materials. We're making history here."

I clip his leash on him, but I still carry him downstairs just so I can get in some extra cuddle time. Bear is nearly five months old and weighs thirty pounds. He's still my little fur baby, and I'm gradually building more arm muscle because of him. Win-win.

As soon as we get outside, Spencer calls over to me, "I told you to let Bear walk more. You carry him too much. He needs to work those little legs."

"He works them every day during our playtime." I set Bear down in the grass and tell him to do his business. Then I walk him over to the garage next to Spencer.

Skylar stands directly behind Gage, watching him take photos of us and directing him for different angles.

He turns to her and offers her my phone. "Sounds like you want to take the pictures."

She smiles sunnily. "You're doing a great job. Keep going. If you can, get the vegetable garden in the background too."

He grumbles something under his breath and takes more pictures. Spencer hams it up, dipping me back over his arm. I laugh. Bear gets excited and jumps up on Spencer.

Spencer pushes Bear off him with one hand and pulls me back upright for a kiss that promises more to come.

I break the kiss and turn to Gage, a little out of breath. "Thanks."

He hands my phone back to me, and I check out the pictures. Skylar's direction really helped. "These are fabulous, thank you."

"Can we demo now?" Gage asks.

Skylar pipes up, "Since I'm here, why don't we just quickly review the design plans together before all the noise and dust?"

Gage looks to the sky, and then his gaze lands on hers, all business. "One-story structure that seats fifty with a reception area, restrooms, storage, and top-of-the-line kitchen. Done. Now get out of my way." That may be the longest sentence I've ever heard him say.

"Excuse me?" Skylar says, her voice hitting a high note.

"Please," he says through his teeth.

"This will go a lot better if you drop the 'tude," she says.

Gage makes a muffled noise I've never heard from him before. I think it's a smothered laugh. And that's definitely a smile. "'Tude? Now that's funny."

Skylar huffs. "You're lucky I'm a pacifist."

Another smothered laugh from Gage.

She turns to me. "Let's go inside the inn to review the plans. I don't think Mr. Grumps here will be much help."

Spencer and I exchange a look. They sound a bit like us in the beginning, and look how great we turned out!

I scoop up Bear and head toward the inn with Skylar. Spencer takes Bear from me, probably to make him walk, but then Bear cuddles against his chest, so he lets him stay there.

"Bye, Miss Perky," Gage calls. "I'll work on that 'tude."

Skylar doesn't bother turning around when she yells back, "See that you do!" Her blue eyes are bright. Does she like Gage, or is that just her usual bright-eyed optimism and enthusiasm?

"He's not so bad," I tell her. "This is our second time working with Gage, and he's competent and professional."

Skylar's chin lifts. "So am I. Don't worry for a moment that I'm going to let him throw me off my game. I'll do my job, and he'll do his."

"Oh, I'm not worried. I just don't want you to be stressed over him. He's great."

"Mmm-hmm," she says noncommittally.

Spencer opens the door for us, and we head inside, going

straight to the dining area, where I laid out the plans for Spencer's restaurant. Brooke worked with Spencer to design it. We have a few paper versions of the plan, as well as the digital one.

"This is your copy to take with you," I tell Skylar, gesturing to the plan. I unclip Bear's leash and let him free in the living room. He loves to sleep under the front window.

Skylar studies the plan for several minutes before turning to Spencer. "What kind of mood are you going for?"

I listen as Spencer and Skylar have an animated conversation over lighting and color. Her enthusiasm is contagious, and I can tell Spencer is getting more excited as they speak. He's gesturing a lot more, his voice rising.

The sound of demolition reaches us as the garage roof is torn down. Gage told me that would go first. He has a dumpster in the street for all the debris. Skylar and Spencer keep talking above the noise until they run out of stuff to go over.

Spencer wraps an arm around my side and pulls me close. "This is going to be awesome."

Skylar beams. "It will be. I'll wait for your kitchen appliance requests. In the meantime, I'm going to pick out some options for you for the main dining area's wall color, upholstery for the chairs, and flooring."

"Can't wait," he says.

"I'll be in touch," she says with a sunny smile and heads out the door.

I turn to him, unable to contain my own sunny smile. "I have a present for you in the kitchen drawer."

"A present for me? But it's not my birthday." He heads over to the kitchen, a bemused expression on his face. "It's the middle of October. Hmm, early Halloween present?"

"What would that be? Candy?"

"I'm hoping a sexy maid's costume. It must be skimpy to fit in a kitchen drawer."

"Hope it fits. Otherwise, you're going to look ridiculous."

He gives me a deadpan look. "For you to wear not me." He opens a drawer and closes it, heading for the next one. "Is it wrapped?"

"Yes, getting warmer."

"I feel like I'm on a treasure hunt."

"You are."

Bear joins him, standing on his hind legs to sniff the open drawer. Spencer pushes his nose away. "You're going to get caught in a drawer." He steps to his left and looks at me.

"Warmer."

There's only one drawer where I could fit the gift. I took half the spices out of it just to hide it there.

He slides open the correct drawer and sucks in air. "It's beautiful." He lifts the Wüsthof knife with a red bow tied around the handle out of the drawer.

"Your favorite chef recommended it." Spencer doesn't follow celebrity chefs; instead he visits top kitchens in the area for inspiration. He's a huge admirer of this chef who works in a nouveau American restaurant in Brooklyn. I've had quite a food awakening thanks to Spencer.

"And that's not all," I say in a gameshow voice.

He sets the knife down. "Why're you getting me presents?" He crosses to me and pulls me close. "Don't you know you're the best gift of all?"

My throat clogs with emotion, my eyes watering. "I promised myself I wouldn't cry." I hug him close and try to contain myself. "I love you so much."

"I love you too." He tilts my chin up. "What's going on?"

I pull away and retrieve the ring from my pocket. Then I go on one knee, holding it up to him. "Spencer Wolf, will you marry me?"

He stares at me. "I've asked you to marry me twice, and you said it couldn't be spontaneous, and it had to be the right place and time. So it's safe to assume that this was planned and is the perfect time."

My heart races. *Is he going to turn me down?* I keep holding up the platinum band with scrollwork, a manly engagement ring. "I hope so?"

He drops to his knees and pulls a diamond ring from his pocket. "Paige Winters, I will happily marry you. Will you happily marry me?"

"Yes!" I'm so happy I burst into tears.

He slides the ring on my finger, and I try to slide his ring on his finger, but everything's blurry through my tears. He helps me, getting his ring on before pulling me to my feet and holding me close against his chest.

His voice rumbles by my ear. "I've been carrying that ring around for weeks, waiting for the right place and time."

I laugh and look up at him. He wipes my tears away with his thumbs. "I just wanted it to feel like it was planned. Like we had intent, not just spur of the moment."

"Oh, it was planned all right. This was a stealth plan to wear you down. Third time's the charm, they say." Even though I'm the one who proposed.

Oh, who cares? It's official! We're getting married!

I throw my arms around him and kiss him passionately, my heart singing. Time ceases to exist. My body hums with an intoxicating combination of love and passion.

He breaks the kiss and scoops up Bear. "Someone wants up. He's climbing my leg."

"You're a natural holding him. Do you, uh, want kids?"

"Yes. I thought I mentioned that. Do you?"

I nod. "The sooner, the better. Two."

"That sounds perfect."

"Yeah?"

"Yeah!"

We laugh and hug again, Bear included, who licks my neck.

"Can you believe we used to fight so much over who was the boss?" I ask.

A smile plays over his lips. "And now you know."

"We're partners, equal bosses."

He cocks his head. "Don't you know me by now, beautiful?"

"Fine. You're the boss in the kitchen. It's not like I *want* to cook."

He gives me a slow sexy smile. "And where else?"

My cheeks flush, which is ridiculous.

He chuckles. "You know. Say it."

"The bedroom, but only because I let you."

He sets Bear down and scoops me up, cradled in his arms. "Because you love it and you love me."

He carries me through the inn, heading toward my apartment.

"This is the beginning of our new life," I say, feeling all mushy. He chased me until I let him catch me. So romantic.

"How's a Christmas Eve wedding sound?" he asks.

I nod, my throat too tight for words.

"We can do it here, small ceremony with only a select few."

"I hadn't thought of an indoor wedding at the inn. It's brilliant! That would encourage couples to show up here for indoor weddings in the winter, too, not just in the summer outside. Do you mind if I ask *Bride Special* to feature us?"

"I'd be insulted if they didn't."

We grin at each other.

"I'm full of brilliant ideas," he says. "Exhibit A, proposing to you until you said yes."

"That *was* brilliant."

"Exhibit B, combining forces to bring our two businesses together."

"Are you sure you don't feel like you missed out on that farm property?"

"I've got room for a huge garden here and access to the best markets around. Besides, you're much more important than owning a cow."

I laugh. He sets me down in front of my apartment door and then pins me against it. My breath stutters out at the lusty look in his eyes.

"No more business," he says against my lips before kissing me.

Bear whines and scratches at the door.

I pull away, let us in, and Bear runs to his toy pile in the corner of the living room, ready to play. He jumps on his squeaky squirrel toy.

Spencer crooks his finger at me. I go to him, and he tosses me over his shoulder, giving my bottom a pat. I sigh happily.

"Let's see what engaged-couple sex is like," he says.

"I hope it's extra romantic," I hint.

He pushes open the door to the bedroom and sets me down. It takes a moment for the head rush to clear, but then I see what he did—rose petals scattered over the bed and a bouquet of red roses on each nightstand.

"When did you do this?" I ask.

"This morning after you went out."

"You said you were going to the market."

"Where they had roses. I wanted to propose to you today, the day we broke ground for our dream life together. And you had the same idea proposing. See what a great match we are?"

I slap a hand over my mouth, trying not to cry.

"Now strip and lie right in the middle of the bed. I've got plans for you."

Here I was planning this proposal thing to go perfectly when he was doing the exact same thing. I drop my hand. "Oh, Spencer."

He scoops me up and puts me in the center of the bed where he ordered me to go. He covers me with his body and cups my jaw. "You're not supposed to cry when I'm seducing you."

"I'm just so happy."

His eyes go soft. "Me too." He kisses me tenderly, and I sigh.

And then he kisses me not so tenderly.

We roll over the petals, caught in a fiery embrace. A perfect match.

Don't miss the next book in the series, *Daring*, where Gage informs Skylar she'll be moving in with him while she works on his home. In her best interests, of course!

*Skylar*

The first time I met Gage Williams, I didn't like him very much. Here's why—he shot down my design idea while I was pitching to potential clients for work on an inn. I'm an interior designer. He's the owner of the construction company in charge of renovations. After a few heated words between us, he had the audacity to call me Miss Perky. Grr...the world needs positive people!

The second time we met, I still didn't like him. No time for an alpha male with a 'tude when I've got a job to do.

The third time, well, that's when he informed me I'd be moving in with him while I work on his home. Wait, I didn't agree to any of that! Just because I'm currently home displaced and broke. Ah, hell.

*Gage*

Skylar is chaos personified, and I bring order to chaos. Especially when a certain Miss Perky is under the delusion that sunny optimism will save the day. Nope. It's me. You're welcome.

Sign up for my newsletter and never miss a new release! kyliegilmore.com/newsletter

## ALSO BY KYLIE GILMORE

**Unleashed Romance <<steamy romcoms with dogs!**

Fetching (Book 1)

Dashing (Book 2)

Sporting (Book 3)

Toying (Book 4)

Blazing (Book 5)

Chasing (Book 6)

Daring (Book 7)

Leading (Book 8)

Racing (Book 9)

Loving (Book 10)

**The Clover Park Series <<brothers who put family first!**

The Opposite of Wild (Book 1)

Daisy Does It All (Book 2)

Bad Taste in Men (Book 3)

Kissing Santa (Book 4)

Restless Harmony (Book 5)

Not My Romeo (Book 6)

Rev Me Up (Book 7)

An Ambitious Engagement (Book 8)

Clutch Player (Book 9)

A Tempting Friendship (Book 10)

Clover Park Bride: Nico and Lily's Wedding

A Valentine's Day Gift (Book 11)

Maggie Meets Her Match (Book 12)

**The Clover Park STUDS series <<hawt geeks who unleash into studs!**

Almost Over It (Book 1)

Almost Married (Book 2)

Almost Fate (Book 3)

Almost in Love (Book 4)

Almost Romance (Book 5)

Almost Hitched (Book 6)

**Happy Endings Book Club Series <<the Campbell family and a romance book club collide!**

Hidden Hollywood (Book 1)

Inviting Trouble (Book 2)

So Revealing (Book 3)

Formal Arrangement (Book 4)

Bad Boy Done Wrong (Book 5)

Mess With Me (Book 6)

Resisting Fate (Book 7)

Chance of Romance (Book 8)

Wicked Flirt (Book 9)

An Inconvenient Plan (Book 10)

A Happy Endings Wedding (Book 11)

**The Rourkes Series <<swoonworthy princes and kickass princesses!**

Royal Catch (Book 1)

Royal Hottie (Book 2)

Royal Darling (Book 3)

Royal Charmer (Book 4)

Royal Player (Book 5)

Royal Shark (Book 6)

Rogue Prince (Book 7)

Rogue Gentleman (Book 8)

**Check out my website for the most up-to-date list of my books:**
**kyliegilmore.com/books**

# ABOUT THE AUTHOR

Kylie Gilmore is the *USA Today* bestselling author of the Unleashed Romance series, the Rourkes series, the Happy Endings Book Club series, the Clover Park series, and the Clover Park STUDS series. She writes humorous romance that makes you laugh, cry, and reach for a cold glass of water.

Kylie lives in New York with her family, two cats, and a nutso dog. When she's not writing, reading hot romance, or dutifully taking notes at writing conferences, you can find her flexing her muscles all the way to the high cabinet for her secret chocolate stash.

Sign up for Kylie's Newsletter and get a FREE book! kyliegilmore.com/newsletter

For text alerts on Kylie's new releases, text KYLIE to the number (888) 707-3025. (US only)

For more fun stuff check out Kylie's website https://www.kyliegilmore.com.

Thanks for reading *Chasing*. I hope you enjoyed it. Would you like to know about new releases? You can sign up for my new release email list at kyliegilmore.com/newsletter. I promise not to clog your inbox! Only new release info, sales, and some fun giveaways.

I love to hear from readers! You can find me at:
    kyliegilmore.com
    Instagram.com/kyliegilmore
    Facebook.com/KylieGilmoreToo
    Twitter @KylieGilmoreToo

If you liked Spencer and Paige's story, please leave a review on your favorite retailer's website or Goodreads. Thank you.

Made in United States
Orlando, FL
07 November 2021

10263112R00109